DENIS HUGH

# BUSH CLAWS

*Complete and Unabridged*

# LINFORD
*Leicester*

First published in Great Britain

First Linford Edition
published 2018

A catalogue record for this book is available
from the British Library.

ISBN 978–1–4448–3667–7

Published by
F. A. Thorpe (Publishing)
Anstey, Leicestershire

Set by Words & Graphics Ltd.
Anstey, Leicestershire
Printed and bound in Great Britain by
T. J. International Ltd., Padstow, Cornwall

This book is printed on acid-free paper

# 1

## Road to the Unknown

The river was broad and shallow, flowing sluggishly west between low banks of mud almost completely covered in a dense mass of mangrove growth and giant tree ferns. The name of the river was the Chargam, and its course lay through some of the most inaccessible country in central Africa. To follow the Chargam on its winding course upstream was to take the road to the unknown, for in spite of modern exploration methods and the use of aircraft, little was known of the land and the hills among which the Chargam rose. In the past, efforts had been made by several explorers to penetrate this part of the country. Some had never been seen again; one had staggered back to civilisation after two long years, insane; the remainder had given up, the task half-completed.

But there are always men to be found

— a small number in every generation who will risk their lives and more to achieve an object. In this case, the object was the survey of the Chargam headwater country. And the man was Rex Brandon, big-game hunter, famous geologist and born student of adventure for its own reward.

It was in the capacity of all three roles that he and a handful of natives were slowly making their way up the river. They travelled in two shallow-draught motor launches with as few stores as possible, but well armed and with a good stock of ammunition for Brandon's various high-velocity sporting rifles — of which he had models to meet every need, from bucks to elephant.

Brandon, leading, the way in the first of the two launches, sat relaxed in the stern sheets, a medium bore rifle across his knees and a shotgun handy beside him. With one hand he grasped the tiller and steered a winding course in and out among the many mud banks and shoals which blocked the Chargam. Cases of stores and geological equipment were stacked forward, while four men squatted none too happily on the mid-ship thwarts. They were uneasy for a number of reasons. For one thing, a lot of stories had reached their ears in the past concerning the nature of the country their employer was intent on penetrating. These were not stories to bolster their courage or reassure them; but their loyalty to Brandon kept them with him.

In the second boat there were only three men with, in charge of them, a tall, raw-boned black man by the name of Scheki. Scheki and Brandon had made a number of safaris together, and knew each other well, each regarding the other with respect. Brandon had on more than one occasion owed his life to the speed of Scheki; while on his part Scheki knew that he would not have been alive had it not been for Brandon's incredible accuracy when it came to using a rifle quickly.

A week ago there had been another man in the party, but the teeming crocodiles of the Chargam River had taken their toll as the boats plugged on and on upstream, heading west with a touch of north towards the mountains far ahead.

Brandon glanced over his shoulder, back at the second boat. Though outwardly he showed no signs of strain, he was as fully aware of the perils that beset their path as the men who travelled with him.

Scheki raised his arm and waved cheerfully. It took a lot to worry him, and he followed Brandon's example of trying not to show his inner feelings. None of the bearers had ever heard him murmur a word which might add to their own instinctive fears.

One of the men in Brandon's boat looked up at his employer and grinned a little sheepishly. '*Bimna*,' he said. 'How much further do we go before making camp?'

Brandon did not answer immediately. Progress had been almost painfully slow, and he wanted to cover as much ground as he could every day. But at the same time he knew it would not be wise to push the men too far.

The day was well advanced, the worst

of the heat being past. Already the blazing orb of the merciless sun had disappeared below the jagged line of the river-bank vegetation. Brandon could feel the lessening of it on his back as he sat in the stern of the launch. Sweat poured from his skin in streams. He would be glad to make camp, he told himself, but he had set his heart on reaching a native kraal which — according to the map he was using — lay a mile or two further upstream from their present position.

'We shall go ashore and make camp soon, Toomba,' he said. 'There is a village I wish to stop at. We reach it soon.'

'It is good, *Inkosi*. Even for us this travel by water is hot and unpleasant.'

'I'd move by night if it wasn't so dangerous,' answered Brandon grimly. 'At least it would be cooler!' He gave a grin and wiped his forehead, tipping his sun helmet to the back of his neck as he did so. Toomba made no comment, but turned to his three companions, and they all talked among themselves in their language.

Brandon narrowed his eyes as he stared

ahead at the oily surface of the slow-flowing river. It was broken here and there by the tell-tale ripples of underwater movement made by crocodiles. Further off, the long jaws of one enormous monster broke the surface and gaped in the air for a moment or two before plunging into the mud again, to churn and thrash about as it went after something the men could not see. Brandon gave an involuntary shudder as he remembered the fate of the boy he had lost a short time before. For once in his life he had been caught unprepared, and by the time he saw the unfortunate man struggling in the water it was too late to save him from the nearest crocodile. Brandon had killed the brute, but that had not brought back the man.

Twisting and winding to the whim of the low-lying ground, the Chargam River flowed down to meet the boats. Brandon kept a keen lookout for traces of the kraal he sought, but it was not until less than an hour before full darkness that he caught sight of the small beehive-shaped huts that lined a break in the mangrove growth at the river's edge. The men saw them at the same time, and an excited discussion broke out among them.

Brandon steered the launch in towards the bank, making a signal to Scheki in the second boat to follow closely. The mud shoals were more numerous hereabouts, and it required all his skill to avoid running aground.

The leading boat was still a hundred yards from the nearest of the riverside village huts when its arrival was heralded by excited shouts from a group of natives who gathered on the edge of the bank and stared in amazement at what they thought a miracle. None of them had ever seen a motor launch before, and the idea of a canoe with no visible paddles to drive it through the water was astounding to them. But curiosity overcame their natural fear of the unknown, and they crowded down to the very edge of the water to get a better sight of the oncoming boats.

Brandon stood up in the stern and raised his arm in a greeting of friendship. He saw it repeated by several of the villagers, but many of the rest hung back, uncertain as to what they ought to do.

It was during this period of indecision that a sudden commotion in the shallow water close to the bank churned the mud into eddies. Next moment the ugly head of one of the great saurian monsters of the river reared itself up, the six-foot jaws gaping open as it lurched towards the nearest group of villagers. Moving with surprising speed on its short, bowed legs, it heaved itself clear of the water.

Brandon wondered what would happen. He did not think any of the men would be in danger, for they must have experienced this kind of thing quite often in the past. Then he changed his opinion hurriedly.

The men had scattered in the face of the crocodile's unexpected rush. Most of them were sprinting well clear of harm's way, but one among them was less fortunate. He did not see the crocodile at first and was slow in making a break. But to make matters worse, he had barely covered ten yards up the gently sloping bank before he let out a wild yell of terror, slipping and falling to the ground. Brandon could not see the exact cause of the disaster, but it was obvious at a glance that unless something happened to prevent it immediately, the vicious jaws of the advancing crocodile would snap shut on the body of the fallen native.

Brandon thought and acted in one single brain impulse. Almost before the unlucky native had hit the ground, Brandon's rifle was up to his shoulder. The crocodile, a grey shape against the dark background of the mangrove, was no easy target. It was sixty or seventy yards from Brandon's boat, but only a matter of three or four feet from the sprawling native. And dusk was falling rapidly.

Brandon judged it perfectly. The sharp report of the high-velocity rifle coincided with the man's scream of fear as he saw his danger. Then the giant crocodile was twisting and thrashing about on the ground, mortally wounded. The fallen man scrambled to his feet in a flash, darting to safety as the creature's armoured tail cut the mud in its death throes. The four men in Brandon's launch were yelling their heads off with excitement, greatly heartened by this exhibition of their employer's prowess. Even

Brandon himself could not hide a smile of satisfaction as he lowered his rifle and watched the crocodile roll over, dead.

Scheki, shouting from the second boat, raised a cheer that was loudly echoed by his three companions.

The main body of natives from the village paused in their flight, turning their heads and taking in the scene. When they realised what had happened, and listened to the excited explanations of the man who had almost been caught by the crocodile, they, too, looked towards the oncoming launches with new respect.

Brandon rapidly brought his boat round in a wide sweep and nosed it in alongside a primitive log jetty, used by the canoes of the tribe. Several of the crude little craft were drawn up on the mud of the shore, while draped from some of the encroaching mangroves were nets.

Brandon wasted no time, in scrambling to dry land, to find himself immediately surrounded by the loudly exclaiming natives, so excited were they at the swift way in which lie had dealt with the crocodile. In the meantime, Scheki's launch had tied up alongside Brandon's. The seven men were standing by, ready to unload at a word from Scheki.

'*Bivana*,' called the headman respectfully, 'do we stay at this place of evil smells?'

Brandon, who had been trying to understand the dialect of his latest hosts, turned his head and grinned. 'Yes,' he answered. 'I can't make these fellows understand yet, but we shall remain here the night. When you've got the gear unloaded go ahead and make camp — clear of the village if possible.'

'*Yebbo, inkosi*,' answered Scheki promptly.

Brandon turned back to the natives. He saw that another small party was hurrying towards them from the kraal itself. Heading them was a wizened little man who was obviously the chief of the tribe. Brandon tried yet another dialect on the men around him, and was rewarded by seeing understanding dawn on their faces. 'Your Chief comes?' he asked.

They agreed that their Chief was indeed coming to greet the great hunter who had saved the life of one among them. It was, for a stranger and a white man, a great thing to do.

Brandon turned to meet the Chief and his followers. With a show of mutual respect and admiration on both sides, Brandon was welcomed to the kraal, leaving his men to take orders from Scheki.

Inside the circle of little beehive huts which formed the village, he and the chief carried out a grave exchange of gifts, tokens of friendship. A handful of brightly coloured beads for the chief from Brandon's pocket; a beautifully cured buck's hide from the Chief. The people of the kraal stood round and watched with marked interest and pleasure. And when it was over, the Chief invited Brandon to be his guest at a meal.

Brandon agreed to the offer; he could see that the Chief was delighted, but also had a feeling that something else was worrying the old man considerably. However, it was not until the two of them were sitting cross-legged outside the Chief's hut, being served by three of the old man's several wives, that Brandon discovered more of what was troubling his host.

'*Bwana mulungu*,' began the Chief in a

grave tone, 'I am indeed relieved that you are here. It was magnificent of you to save the life of one of my worthless people from the crocodile, but it is not for that I am relieved.' Brandon sensed that the Chief did not quite know how to tell whatever was in his mind.

'Speak freely, Chief,' he said reassuringly. 'I am ready to help you if there is any trouble that threatens your kraal.' At the back of his mind he was wondering if he could get any information regarding the deeper interior from the people whose guest he now was.

'I speak then,' said the Chief. 'It is this way: a few days ago two white men came to my kraal. They were both close to death's door, and I did not think they would live, for they seem to have passed through many great dangers. They are ill of the white man's sickness, malaria. My doctors have tried to cure them, *inkosi*, but their medicines are not for white men.'

Brandon listened without interruption, but his pulse quickened for all that. When the old man stopped, he said: 'You must take me to these white men, Chief, for I have the medicines they need and can cure them. Then I will learn their story. You are a good man to care for them.'

'*Bwana*, they are men and I could not watch them die.'

As soon as the meal was over, Brandon indicated that he would like to be taken to the hut where the sick whites were lodged. The Chief himself led the way, and Brandon called for Scheki to bring his medicine chest from the camp just outside the kraal.

Stooping low to enter the stuffy little mud hut, Brandon and the Chief stood looking down on a pair of rough beds made from interlaced lianas and hides. A black-eyed native woman was squatting on her haunches between the two beds. She rose at once when she saw the Chief, bowing to the ground and touching her forehead as she did so. On the two beds were the white men. Their eyes were closed, and to Brandon's experienced glance it was plain that they were both going through a severe bout of malaria. The fever would have to run its course, he thought, but he had drugs in his chest that would speed it considerably.

'They're bad,' he said quietly. 'Lucky to have reached your village, Chief. I will tend them now.'

Scheki appeared with the medicine chest and stood waiting for orders, his eyes on the two men.

Brandon stared down at them. Their breathing was thin and shallow, their faces drawn and yellowish-looking, with bright spots of colour on the cheek-bones. One was a grey-haired man of middle age, small and thin; the other was in his twenties, a young blond giant with well-cut features. As Brandon turned and opened the medicine chest, he stirred in his semi-conscious state, muttering to himself.

Brandon selected quinine, took Scheki's water canteen, and prepared a draft for both the invalids. He was bending down to force some between the younger man's lips when a tumble of words reached his ears. The young man suddenly wakened, grasping his arm with thin hard fingers and holding it in a feverish grip.

'Lion!' he whispered violently. 'A woman with a lion! They'll get us for sure! The natives got us, but we broke away. It's the woman, man! A white woman. And that damned lion!' His head suddenly lolled over sideways. He was exhausted again, spent by the force of his swift return to consciousness.

'Take it steady, old man,' advised Brandon. He knew the man had spoken in a state of delirium, but even so his odd words had brought a sense of excitement to Brandon's mind. He had heard men say strange things before when they were under the spell of malaria. Sometimes the things they said were nothing more than fantasy; but often enough they were true.

Brandon exchanged a glance with Scheki and the Chief of the tribe. Scheki had understood; the Chief had not. 'You heard that?' said Brandon quietly. Scheki nodded wordlessly. 'I wonder how they landed up in this god-forsaken district,' mused Brandon a moment later. 'They'll be sensible by the morning probably, then we'll learn a little more.'

'It will be interesting, *bwana*,' answered Scheki in a non-committal tone. 'We sleep now, yes?'

16

Brandon rose to his feet. 'Yes,' he said. 'I'll stay in here with these two fellows just to be on the safe side in case they come round again.' Scheki nodded. 'It looks as if we shall have to hold up a while here till they're fit enough to talk. Tell the rest of the men and see that they don't pick a quarrel with the kraalmen. They've shown us hospitality, remember.'

'It shall be, *inkosi*,' Scheki replied gravely.

Brandon was left alone with the two sick men. Full darkness had come outside. A woman brought a crude oil lamp and set it down on the floor of the hut. Brandon squatted with his back against the side of the low doorway. He lit his pipe and smoked it thoughtfully, glancing every now and again at the two restless figures on the beds.

# 2

## Brandon Accepts a Challenge

The night passed uneventfully, though not in complete silence. Down by the river, Scheki and the men were enjoying the local hospitality. Native beer appeared to be flowing freely; and if the singing that was going on was any indication, the men of the safari party were now close friends with their hosts. Brandon smiled to himself. He was not worried about it. Scheki would see that the revelry did not go too far; and since the party was unlikely to move on the next day, it did not matter a great deal if there were some thick heads among the men.

He himself spent a little time in conversation with the old Chief and a couple of his headmen, but he did not attempt to pump them for information yet awhile. It would be time enough to loosen their tongues when they got to know him well and he had discovered if there was any truth in the wild talk of the delirious man.

When at last he turned in, everything was quiet apart from the constant sounds of the jungle life around the kraal. As he rolled himself in a blanket and fastened his mosquito net, his ears picked out the dozens of different night birds and tiny creatures of nocturnal habit as they scuttled about in the undergrowth that pressed in close at the back of the village.

When daylight dawned on the river and the kraal, there was bustle and movement, a great deal of shouting and the chatter of the women as they prepared the morning meal. Some of the tribesmen set off on a hasty hunting trip, returning in an hour or two with several jungle pigs to their credit.

Scheki came to the village from the camp shortly after Brandon had awakened. He was in high spirits and told of the night's festivity. By then Brandon had seen to the two sick whites, giving them medicine and noting with satisfaction that already their fever was abating.

Scheki brought Brandon's food and coffee. It was while he was setting it down that a weak voice called from inside the little hut. Brandon hurried in.

The first thing he saw was that the younger of the two whites was sitting up on his bed and staring about with bright, hollow eyes as if not understanding where he was. Then he saw Brandon and Scheki. The faintest grin of pleasure crossed his features as Brandon came towards him. 'Hello there,' he whispered faintly. 'I seem to have lost every ounce of strength I ever had.'

'Malaria, son,' said Brandon grimly. 'I shouldn't try yourself too much. You'll be fine in a day or two, so just relax. Lucky we found you here.'

The young man nodded ruefully. 'It's coming back to me now,' he muttered, shaking his head and rubbing a thin hand across his pale, drawn face. 'How long have I been here?'

'I can't say for certain,' answered Brandon. 'I and my party arrived yesterday. You were both in pretty bad shape then, but the dope seems to have worked on you well.'

The young man fell silent at that. Then: 'Give me some water, please,' he said. 'I've got to do a lot of talking before the old man comes to.'

'I shouldn't advise it,' said Brandon, handing him a mug of water and quinine.

'Too important to keep to myself,' was the answer.

Brandon grinned in spite of himself. 'All about a white woman and a lion?' he murmured gently.

The young man blinked and stared at him. 'How did you know?' he asked incredulously.

'You yammered a bit in your sleep last night,' Brandon told him. 'Don't worry about it.'

'But I've got to!' The man leant forward on one elbow, speaking quietly yet forcefully, straining to put his words over convincingly without raising his voice too much. 'Listen, my name's Dorton — Mike Dorton. I'm the old man's secretary and assistant.'

'Who is he, anyway?'

'One of the cleverest guys I've ever

known. He's what people call an inventor. Sometimes I think he's crazy, but he's certainly clever when it comes to electronics — that's what brought us to this state of affairs.'

Brandon pushed him gently back onto the bed. 'Take it in easy stages, Mike,' he warned. 'You'll wear yourself out before you start.'

'His name is Litzgor,' went on Dorton slowly. 'There's foreign blood in him somewhere, of course, but it must have been a long time ago. Jan Litzgor is as British as I am. He invents things and then insists on trying them out under the most frightful conditions he can find.'

'What particular invention brought you to Africa?'

But Mike Dorton was cagey as well as communicative. He shook his head. 'Sorry,' he said disarmingly, 'but that's not my secret to pass on to anyone — unless the old man passes out, which I doubt. He's tough! It was his latest toy which prompted him to come to these parts; that's all I'm at liberty to say — beyond the fact that he's lost it way up there among the mountains. If it hadn't been for malaria getting him, I'd never have persuaded him to beat a retreat.' He broke off and gave a weary smile. 'And that was in spite of the natives and the white woman and her blasted lion!' he added wryly. 'He'd have stayed and fought the lot till they killed him, I think. We were lucky to get away with our lives as it was.'

Brandon frowned as the other man stopped. Then he glanced across at the troubled and restlessly sleeping figure of the middle-aged inventor, Litzgor. 'Tell me,' he said to Dorton, 'whereabouts did this happen? How long were you wandering about before you found this kraal? And what is all this business of a white woman with a lion?'

Mike Dorton sat up again, took another drink of the quinine and water mixture, and then said: 'I thought you'd be interested. Jan and I set out to test his precious old invention about seven months ago. The old man was so keen on secrecy that no one knew of our departure; nor did they know where we intended to go. Even I didn't know that, or I'd have pointed out the folly of penetrating unexplored country without proper precautions and a strong force of armed men. All we had was a little safari of four bearers and as small a quantity of equipment as possible.

'Needless to say, we ran into trouble soon enough. Two of the men were killed during a washout in the rainy season. Soon after that, we were attacked by natives and so lost the other two. That left the old man and myself — and his invention! But it didn't save us; it's not that kind of toy.

'He insisted on keeping to plan, and the two of us — just like a pair of idiots — walked slap into a second small army of natives. Fortunately for us, there was a narrow gorge between our enemies and us. It held them up for just long enough to give us a chance to escape the worst of it, but even so they nearly had us.'

He hesitated, watching Brandon as if wondering whether or not the tall bronzed man would believe him. Then: 'You can believe me or not,' he went on more slowly, 'but there was a white woman with that bunch of natives. She was a mighty handsome creature, too, and she looked almost as willing to kill us as they did.'

Brandon smiled a little. 'And she had a tame lion?' he murmured.

'You don't believe me, do you?' countered Dorton hotly. 'But it's true, I tell you! Yes, she did have a lion with her. She definitely did, man! And I heard her speak to it several times, what's more. She had that brute under her thumb just as much as she did the natives.'

Brandon looked at Dorton hard. He did not know whether the young man was telling the truth or was still labouring under the fantasy his brain had kindled during a spell of delirium. 'How was this woman dressed?' he asked suddenly.

Dorton frowned. Then: 'Breeches and boots,' he said. 'But her shirt was gone and she was wearing a leopard-skin bodice affair.' He grinned. 'She wasn't bad to look at, I tell you, but it wouldn't have surprised me at all if I'd seen a pair of horns sprouting from her forehead!

She must have been a proper devil.'

'She's still alive, though?'

Dorton nodded quickly. 'As far as I know,' he said. 'The last we saw of her, she was raving at her men and urging them on to slaughter us. It was only the gorge between that saved us. Some of them got across and chased us. Jan tripped and fell. That's when he lost his invention. It flew out of his hands and there wasn't time to find it again. We simply ran for our lives and got away — which was all we cared about by then. How it was that they didn't track us down, I don't know, but we never saw a trace of them after that.'

Brandon said nothing for a few seconds. He sat on the side of Dorton's crude bed and rubbed his chin thoughtfully as the young man watched him. Then, just as Brandon was on the point of saying something, there was a move from the other bed, and Jan Litzgor opened his eyes in a bleary fashion. The malaria fever had taken its toll of him to a greater extent than on Dorton, who, being a younger man, was better able to throw it off. But for all that, Litzgor began talking.

'You've been giving away my secrets!' he said accusingly, glaring at Dorton with hostility in his fever-bright eyes.

'Don't be a fool,' retorted the younger man. 'This chap saved our lives. I haven't told him anything you wouldn't have done yourself. You take it easy.'

Litzgor relaxed, leaning back and watching Brandon with marked suspicion in spite of what Dorton said. But at last Brandon broke the tension.

'Look,' he said quietly, 'I'm not after your secrets, sir. I merely happened on this village and was told by the Chief that a couple of sick whites were lying here. Since then, I've done what I could for you. Dorton has told me something of your experiences, and I must say I sympathise with you. If there's anything I can do, you've only to let me know.'

'Your name?' demanded the older man tersely. 'What are you doing in this part of Africa?'

Brandon hid a smile. He did not envy Dorton his job as Litzgor's secretary. It must have been somewhat trying at times.

'I'm Rex Brandon,' he explained. 'If you haven't heard of me, I'm a geologist and big-game hunter. What I am doing here is a side-issue, but I'll tell you. I'm up in this country — which has not been thoroughly explored by whites before — with the object of exploration and assessing the mineral possibilities of the headwater country of the Chargam. You don't need to know any more.'

Jan Litzgor seemed oddly pacified by the information. 'Brandon,' he said, 'I owe you an apology. Please accept our gratitude for all you have done.'

'Forget it,' said Brandon quietly. 'I can understand your feelings. And now I suggest you rest, both of you. I shall not be leaving the village until you're fit enough to continue your way back to civilisation.' He got to his feet and turned to the hut entrance. 'My head man will remain within call. If there is anything you need, don't hesitate to ask him for it.'

They thanked him and he left, making his way down to the camp to see how things were going. There he found the

Chief of the tribe deep in consultation with one of the men regarding some of Brandon's rifles, which seemed to fascinate the old man enormously. It was not the first time he had seen such weapons, he explained, but he had never had a chance to examine one before.

When Brandon loaded a small bore gun and allowed him to fire it, there was no limit to the Chiefs delight, especially as the majority of the villagers had witnessed the performance. To Brandon, it was another step towards making the chief his friend in order to gain information about the interior, for he knew that the man would be cautious in what he said.

During the day, Brandon went out with a few of the men and tribesmen on a short hunting trip. Game was plentiful, and the additional food brought back to the kraal and the camp was welcome. Shortly after the midday meal, he made his way to the hut where the sick men were lodged.

Scheki greeted him at the entrance, to say that they were considerably better and had been talking a great deal during the morning.

Brandon nodded. 'Glad to hear it,' he said cheerfully.

'*Bwana*,' murmured Scheki, 'I think they do not want to return to civilisation. They talk much of going back to find what was lost. They do not realise I understand what they say, but it is possible that they ask you to help them.'

Brandon grinned and laid a hand on Scheki's shoulder. 'You have long ears, Scheki,' he said.

'It is good!' The tall man grinned broadly as he nodded violently. Then he slipped away and left his employer alone at the door of the hunt.

Going inside, he paused and looked round. 'My man tells me you're both a lot better,' he said.

Jan Litzgor sat up in bed. He still looked pale and drawn, but the light of fever had left his eyes and his cheeks were less sunken. As for Mike Dorton, the change in him was even more marked.

'Thanks to you, Brandon. We are on the mend,' said Litzgor gravely.

Brandon sat down on a canvas chair he had sent for earlier on. He felt for his pipe and filled it carefully, not looking at either of the men. At length: 'A few days' rest and you'll be fit to travel downstream to a more comfortable place than this,' he said slowly. 'I've no doubt I could manage if I lent you one of my launches to make the journey. How would that suit you?' He raised his head and peered at them in turn.

Litzgor smiled knowingly. 'Perhaps it wouldn't suit us to go downstream, Brandon,' he murmured.

'Oh?'

'Dorton told you we had lost something of priceless value when we escaped from the natives among the mountains. It is my earnest desire to recover that thing.'

Brandon shook his head doubtfully. 'Sounds a tall order to me,' he said. 'There are only two of you, and from what I gather, this white woman and her lion can call on an army of men to do what she wants.'

Dorton said nothing, but bit his lower lip.

Litzgor frowned. 'You do not know me, Brandon,' he answered. 'I am a man of determination. If I say I am going back after my invention, there will be no stopping me! I was under the impression that you yourself were penetrating the self-same country in which we met disaster. Am I to understand now that you are too much of a coward to let us go with you?' His eyes were keen and accusing as he spoke.

Brandon grinned and puffed at his pipe for a moment in silence. 'So that's your idea, is it?' he said. 'I'm not at all sure that it's wise, sir. There are many unknown dangers to be faced, and I wouldn't like to be responsible for your safety. With me, it's a different matter. I'm a free agent and can go wherever my men will follow, but I go at my own risk.'

Litzgor compressed his mouth into a tight hard line. 'Hand me a drink, Brandon,' he said. 'I hadn't thought you'd take this attitude. I must say I'm a little disappointed in you!'

Brandon hid a smile as he reached out with a canteen of fresh water. His eyes met those of Dorton's for an instant, who closed one eye in a barely perceptible wink. Brandon said: 'Disappointed, sir? I was only pointing out the danger of what you suggest.'

'Then I challenge you to prove it!' he snapped. 'Are you afraid of taking us with you to the headwater country?'

Brandon got to his feet and thrust his hands into his pockets, his pipe clenched between his strong teeth. 'No,' he said quietly. 'I'm not afraid. If you're daring me to take you along, that's your funeral. I'm ready enough to accept your challenge — and I'll try to get back that darned invention for you!'

Silence greeted his words for a second or two, then both men burst out, thanking him at the same time. Brandon shook his head. 'Wait till we get it,' he warned. 'It may not be so simple!'

# 3

## The Waterfall

Three weeks had passed since Brandon agreed to take Jan Litzgor and Mike Dorton with him when he continued his voyage up the treacherous Chargam River. Several days of that time had been taken up at the kraal of the friendly tribe, but in spite of all Brandon's blandishments he had not been able to gain any real information regarding the hazards of the land he would be entering. The old Chief had been extremely cagey when it came to speaking of the mountains in the distance, and in the end Brandon had given it up as a bad job, knowing that he would never break down the native superstition about them. They and all the dangers they contained were looked on as bad *ju-ju*, and that was that. All he had to go on was the word of Dorton that somewhere ahead on the route they would follow, there were hostile natives under the control of a white woman who kept a lion.

And so the time had passed. The launches had been checked and the stores rearranged. Brandon had hunted nearly every day from the vicinity of the kraal. Scheki and the rest of the men had grown fat from their hosts' open-handedness; and Litzgor and Dorton had fully recovered from their bout of malaria.

Now the whole party was far upstream from the kraal, and still driving deeper and deeper into the almost unexplored country from which the Chargam flowed. For ease of control and division of the men, Brandon had kept Jan Litzgor in the leading boat with him, while Mike travelled with Scheki in the second craft. The two men had been armed with Brandon's rifles, of which there were enough to go round. Brandon himself was not displeased to have company, for now that they were all together in the venture, even Litzgor proved himself to be a cheerful character, though there were moments when his quick temper tried

Brandon a little. Mike Dorton he liked immensely, and the two of them had long talks when the boats were moored against the bank and camp had been made for the night.

The broad sluggish river was gradually changing now. Its banks, which before had been wide and flat, clad in mangrove growth, now narrowed and were steeper. Jungle vegetation still came almost to the water's edge, while here and there they saw jutting outcrops of rock thrusting through the dense foliage. The current, too, was more rapid, and the number of crocodiles less.

'It looks as if we're entering the higher ground, Jan,' said Brandon one morning.

Jan Litzgor nodded thoughtfully. Sitting in the stern of the launch with Brandon, he made a quaint figure, for his hair had grown long in the jungle and his bush garb was ragged. There was a five-day growth of stubble on his chin. He had announced his intention of growing a beard, much to the amusement of his two white companions, but was obviously serious about it.

'Yes,' he said, 'we were so riddled with

fever when we arrived at the village that I can't for the life of me tell you which way we came, but it was certainly in among the hills ahead that we met with trouble. According to your map, our route came into the headwater country from a different direction to this, but it comes to the same thing. It's in that hill country we want to be.'

'Well, it suits me well enough,' answered Brandon. 'I'm making this trip myself with the object of testing for mineral potential. Have you any idea what it's like up here? All strange territory to me, but there might be something worth noting.'

Litzgor was silent for a moment. Then: 'I know nothing of geological research,' he answered flatly.

Brandon frowned a little. He was on the point of saying something more when he decided not to. It struck him as extremely odd that Jan should close up at the mention of mineral research. If Mike hadn't said that his employer was a first-rate mineralogist, he would have thought nothing of it; but knowing that, he was interested in spite of himself. Why, he wondered curiously, did Litzgor not wish to discuss the mineral potential of the country ahead? It was a puzzle that had him guessing; but it was not one which was to find an answer for some considerable time to come.

'Shall we be able to carry on right to the head of the river?' queried Jan, changing the subject abruptly. It was almost as if he wanted to take Brandon's mind off the subject of minerals.

'I doubt it,' Brandon answered slowly. 'Before long we shall find that the slope of the ground rises considerably. It's not too bad at the moment, but even so the current is speeding up a lot. There'll be rapids ahead, with perhaps a fall or two thrown in. We can cope with rapids if they aren't too fierce, but these boats are too heavy to carry by porterage when we come to a fall.'

Litzgor nodded disappointedly. 'I was hoping it would not be so,' he said. 'We should have to continue on foot when the river becomes impracticable, I suppose?'

'That's the general idea. I shouldn't let it worry you!'

'I am not in the habit of worrying, Brandon.'

'Fine.'

That night when they tied up against the lowest part of the bank they could find, it was quite a difficult feat to get the camp gear ashore, for the level of the banks had risen a great deal since morning. The flow of the river, too, was very much swifter than previously.

When Brandon lay in his tent before going to sleep, he reflected that the future was an uncertain thing to bet on, and made even more so by the company he was keeping. He smiled to himself, listening to the murmuring of the jungle around him as night clamped down. And while he was listening, his keen ears attuned themselves to another sound; it was a distant roar, dull and changeless, almost a rumble. He knew what it was all right, and knew that probably tomorrow they would have to leave the boats and take to the narrow creature-made paths of the jungle. It was not a prospect he looked forward to, but he knew it to be unavoidable.

With the chatter and clamour of the river banks by day, it was impossible to catch the distant murmur of the waterfall. Brandon said nothing about having heard it. Scheki, however, had not missed the sinister rumble, but had also kept it to himself.

The two boats covered a fair distance that day, but all the time the Chargam was getting narrower, deeper and swifter. On more than one occasion, ugly rocks jutted up from the water, causing eddies and undercurrents which were minor rapids in themselves. And on either side of the river itself, the ground was rising in jungle-covered slopes which themselves were blotted out by towering trees that closed in the range of vision of the men and limited them to the sides of the gorge through which the launches chugged.

Finding a place to land for the night was no easy task, and when at length they did, it was to lie uncomfortably on a bare shelf or rock just above water level.

'This is the last day we'll use the river,' said Brandon regretfully. The murmur of the waterfall had by this time risen to a bellow of sound. The men found that they had to raise their voices above it.

Mike shrugged his shoulders cheerfully. 'Can't be helped, skipper!' he said with a grin. 'I'm as good as the next man when it comes to trekking.'

'No doubt,' replied Brandon dryly. 'But it cuts down our speed considerably. We'll be lucky if we make five miles a day through the stuff up there.' He jerked his head at the dense foliage crowning the sharply sloping sides of the river bed.

'I seem to remember hearing a waterfall in the distance when we were making our escape from those natives,' mused Jan Litzgor thoughtfully. 'If it's the one ahead of us, it looks as if we can't be very far from our goal. Impossible to say from where we are whether we're in among the hills or not.'

'I think we are,' said Brandon. 'But as you say, it's hard to tell. One can't see more than a few yards through this jungle on the banks. We'll know more tomorrow.'

But the morrow brought them little more than heart-breaking labour and a desperate battle for their lives.

Just as Brandon had predicted, their way was barred before many hours by a tumbling torrent of water. It thundered down in a deafening cascade from high on a rocky ridge. Dense jungle foliage, bright green from the moisture, hid everything except the fall itself. The two boats were tossed about in a mass of surging, broken water against the current of which their engines were almost useless.

'No good!' yelled Brandon, signalling back to Dorton and Scheki. 'We'll have to make land and find a place to leave the boats.' He was shouting in Litzgor's ear to make him understand.

The inventor nodded wordlessly, then mouthed something that Brandon did not catch. Brandon turned the launch towards the nearest feasible-looking spot on the bank. A small inlet, worn by some stream during the rainy season, offered temporary harbourage for both the boats. Here they were firmly secured out of harm's way. Brandon hoped they would still be safe by the time he and his companions returned from the rest of the trek; he saw no reason why they should not be. The question of stores was fully discussed between them. It was finally decided to travel light, taking only the bare essentials for life in the jungle, as well as all the weapons and a plentiful supply of ammunition.

It was an hour after midday when they set off, scrambling up the steeply sloping bank and then sticking as close as they could to the line of the river. But progress was difficult. The jungle, thicker than ever now on account of the extra moisture in the air, seemed intent on keeping them back. The ground was rising at an acute angle, and Brandon was forced to make a considerable detour when they eventually reached the base of the green-walled cliff over which the river tumbled. The thick green shadows of the jungle were growing darker by the time they finally breasted the rise and hacked their way through to the bank of the Chargam at its new level.

'We'd better start looking for a place to camp,' suggested Dorton. He mopped his brow. They were all sweating profusely, for the atmosphere was like that of a steam oven. Even the tough men found the going hard, and Scheki was quick to back up Dorton, adding in an aside to Brandon that the men were growing uneasy among themselves.

'They have never seen such jungle as this, *inkosi*,' he whispered. 'It is full of evil spirits, and sometimes I think they are right.'

Brandon smiled, but he did not take the warning as lightly as it seemed. He knew that unless he and Scheki handled the men with the greatest care, they would desert in a body. Their memories were too short to stand up in the face of the unknown despite all they knew of their employer's powers.

'Scheki,' said Brandon slowly, 'there is no other evil but the fangs and claws of animals. You and I know we can deal with them. Make the others realise it, too. If they leave us it will be bad, and on their own they would quickly perish. Make them understand it.'

'*Yebbo, baas*,' murmured Scheki with a grave nod of his woolly head. 'It shall be. They will remain.'

With evening rapidly closing in and the short tropic twilight coming on, the three whites hurriedly selected a spot where the undergrowth was less dense than anywhere else nearby.

'We camp,' shouted Brandon. 'Scheki, get a site clear of thorn and pitch the tents.'

The men hurriedly dumped their loads, and in a very short space of time their machetes had levelled the foliage in a wide circle. In this the party settled down.

Brandon stretched himself on the ground with his back against the bole of a thick-barked *mopani* tree, the branches of which spread out above his head like a giant umbrella. Mike Dorton flung himself down a yard or so away, while Litzgor squatted on one of the cases of stores and let his head sag forward in his hands. He was feeling the strain of the laborious trek.

A cooking fire was soon lit and the preparation of a meal underway. Brandon and Dorton started cleaning their guns; Litzgor seemed to be lost in some reverie of his own. Mike spoke to him once, but was ignored. He winked at Brandon and carried on with what he was doing. Scheki came up to announce that the meal was ready. The two men rose to their feet. Brandon looked round, taking in the scene of the camp, with the dark green foliage gleaming in the flickering light of the fire. He saw Scheki's grinning face; the glistening skin of the men; the pallor of Litzgor's features and the brightness of his eyes as he looked up. If the man wasn't careful, thought Brandon, he would have a recurrence of malaria, which would be a nuisance under the circumstances. Then he stiffened, seeing something that had no part in the camp scene.

'Mike!' he shouted urgently. 'Look out, man!' Dorton whirled round. He was several yards from where Brandon stood.

'What — ?' he began, startled.

But Brandon had grabbed his rifle and was aiming at a spot in the undergrowth just to one side of Dorton. Even as Mike turned round, the rifle shattered the twilight silence. Dorton hurled himself to one side, thinking for an instant that Brandon had gone crazy and meant to kill him. Then Brandon was racing forward, ready for a second shot.

46

'What the devil?' demanded Dorton, finding his voice again.

'Snake!' snapped Brandon. He reached the undergrowth with Dorton close at his heels. Litzgor was coming after them fast. The men were huddled together near the campfire, frightened by the sudden activity.

Brandon halted and stood looking down at the long body of the biggest snake he had ever seen; also it was a variety he did not recognise, which troubled him somewhat.

'My God!' whispered Dorton, aghast. 'It must be twenty feet long!'

'I've never seen anything like it,' Brandon admitted.

Dorton turned his head, peering into the blackness of the undergrowth. 'Let's hope there aren't any more like it,' he muttered uneasily.

Brandon's sharp ears picked out a rustling not far away. 'Watch it!' he said curtly. His gun swept round, but even so he was almost too late. A second of the monstrous reptiles slithered into view, making straight for the spot at which they were gathered. Only Brandon was armed.

His rifle crashed again. The enormous length of the snake curled and twisted as the bullet struck its neck. One end of it lashed round and caught Litzgor about the ankles, throwing him to the ground. Brandon shouted to Mike to stand out of the way, then he fired again, perilously close to Litzgor. At the same instant, Scheki arrived on the scene with a second gun which he thrust into Dorton's hands. Then he gave a squeal of involuntary fear. Fully a dozen of the giant reptiles were converging on the three whites and himself.

Brandon saw them, too, while Dorton and Scheki dragged Litzgor clear of the one he started shooting at the others.

Several of the men pulled themselves together and came into the fight, using short hunting spears they always carried. Then Dorton and Litzgor were throwing in their weight against the swift attack of the great snakes.

But the party were not to escape entirely unscathed. Just as Brandon fired at one of the snakes, it twisted aside so swiftly that his bullet went wide in the gloom. Next instant there was a scream of agony and terror from one of the men. Fastening round his waist, the reptile dragged him down, slowly crushing him in its tenuous coils. Brandon held his breath in suspense, for the body of the man was right in his line of fire. He dare not squeeze the trigger. Scheki hurled himself forward, an upraised machete in his right hand, slashing and hacking at the coils of the serpent in an effort to free the unfortunate captive.

But by the time he succeeded, the man had been strangled by a coil round his throat. Nor could anyone give him immediate attention, for they had their work cut out in the fight against the remaining snakes. Where they had all come from, Brandon never knew; but in the heat of the battle it seemed as if they would never stop coming. Between them, when it was over, they found they had slaughtered nearly twenty of the monstrous reptiles, apart from wounding a great many more and driving them off.

'That's the lot, I think,' Dorton grated between his teeth. He peered into the undergrowth, straining his eyes in the gloom.

There was no further movement in the scrub and thorn of the jungle around them. Brandon wiped the sweat from his face, reloading his rifle in case of another emergency.

The men were gathered round their dead comrade. Scheki stood by, glancing at the snakes where they lay on the ground. There was a haunting fear in his sombre eyes as the firelight caught them.

Brandon bent and examined one of the monsters. He was oddly troubled by its appearance, for there was something so primeval about it that it might have slithered from another world. 'I think they're amphibious creatures,' he murmured to Dorton. 'Frankly, I've never come across a thing like this in all my jungle experience.'

'Nor I,' answered Dorton in a worried tone. 'What have we landed ourselves in for, Rex?'

'It's too late to turn back,' put in Litzgor quickly.

Brandon met his eyes. 'I've no intention of turning back,' he said. 'I suggest we clear these things off our campsite and turn in for the night. We'll have to mount a continuous guard, of course.'

'That goes without saying,' commented Litzgor. 'Thank you, Brandon, for saving my life. I almost forgot it.'

Brandon grinned. 'All in the day's work,' he said.

They set the men dragging the snakes from the camp. The man who had been killed was buried with as much ceremony as possible under the prevailing conditions, and the camp slowly settled down to sleep.

The three whites took turns on guard, listening in an effort to pick out anything unusual among the normal sounds of the night. Brandon sat watch for the last two hours of darkness. He leant against a *baobab* tree, his rifle nestling in the crook of his arm, eyes keen and alert as he glanced continuously round. The men were sleeping on the far side of the camp. Nearer to him were the three tents used by himself and the others. The fire had died down to a mass of glowing embers, but its faint radiance still shed sufficient light for Brandon to make out the slumbering shapes of the men. The slightest movement beyond the fringe of the camp took his attention. He tensed himself, ready for anything.

At one moment he saw the movement. Then something gave a high-pitched twang of sound. It was followed immediately by a groaning cry from one of the slumbering men. His body reared up and flopped back inert, a long arrow buried in his chest.

Brandon raced forward, shouting an alarm. There was no indication of where the concealed killer might be. All sign of movement had vanished in the undergrowth, and the sudden yelling of the startled men covered what noise there might have been to give him a line. It was obviously useless trying to go after the unseen marksman in darkness.

Scheki, Dorton and Litzgor crowded round him. The men stared unbelievingly at their dead companion.

'*Bwana*,' said Scheki soberly, 'this is evil country. It is death that strikes from the unknown. Someone does not welcome us here.'

'Don't let the men hear you say that,' said Brandon.

'They are saying it already, *inkosi*.'

'But who the devil killed him like that?' demanded Mike in a querulous tone. 'It's not like African natives to creep up at night and kill so stealthily. They usually make a song and dance about it.'

'Just what I was thinking,' put in Litzgor thoughtfully. 'Oh, well, nothing we can do about it except keep our eyes open every minute of the day and night.'

There was no more sleep for anyone that night, and by morning the temper of the five remaining men was very uneasy. The fact was that they were badly frightened. Brandon had qualms as to whether they would stick to him, but he felt that if anyone could persuade them to, it was Scheki.

They set off again shortly after dawn, conscious of a growing tension in the atmosphere.

# 4

## Beware the Ruined City!

Brandon and Scheki examined the ground before leaving the site of the tragic camp. Just as Brandon had expected, they found the spot at which the man had stood when he fired his arrow and killed their hapless colleague. His prints were easy enough to follow in the line of retreat, too, but Brandon decided that it would not be worth their while to attempt it.

Scheki looked up from where he knelt on the ground. 'Him big native, *bwana*,' he muttered. 'See, wide feet, very long as well. Tall man. who run swiftly with very long strides.'

Brandon nodded. 'You're right,' he agreed. 'Come on, Scheki, let's get moving. The further we get from this place the better. The men don't like it, I know, and what with giant snakes and unseen murderers, I'm not surprised.'

Scheki darted a glance round, then rose to his feet. 'It is well that we go, *inkosi*,' he said quietly. 'The men are unhappy.'

Brandon turned away and joined up with Litzgor and Mike, who were supervising the packing of equipment and loading up of the men.

The path wound on through the twists and turns of the steeply rising ground. For the most part the white men were compelled to cut their way through, and their route was rigidly dictated by the jungle-clad outcrops of towering rock through which they passed. Sometimes they were forced aside from the general direction chosen; at others there was no other way to go.

At a necessarily slow rate of progress the party advanced, with Brandon and Dorton in the lead. Litzgor brought up the rear, with the men and Scheki in between. Scheki acted as trail-breaker to Brandon when the path became tangled. For hours they plodded on, torn by thorn scrub and sweating under the steamy heat of the green hell through which they forced their way.

It was late afternoon when Brandon came to a halt in front of a particularly dense wall of greenery. He stood there peering through the foliage with a puzzled frown on his face. Mike Dorton stopped beside him.

'What's the trouble?' he queried. 'As if I didn't know!'

Brandon smiled bleakly. 'Take a look at that,' he said. Dorton bent and squinted through the leaves and scrub.

'Stonework!' he said in amazement. 'What — ?'

Brandon cut him short by forcing a way through the dense undergrowth and laying bare a section of what was obviously a man-made wall of cut stones.

'In this place!' muttered Mike.

'Long-lost civilisation,' said Brandon. He turned as Jan Litzgor came up beside them, a puzzled expression on his features.

'Seems that we aren't the only people to have penetrated this district. This stuff was never erected by men.'

'I wouldn't be too sure of that,' replied Brandon. 'We have no conception of what their capabilities were several thousand years ago, remember. They might have had a form of civilisation entirely beyond our comprehension.'

Mike Dorton rubbed his chin in a ruminative fashion. 'I can't see that it makes a great deal of difference. We can at least make use of the place as a camp site for tonight. Frankly, I feel like taking a rest; this jungle gets me down at times.'

Brandon grinned. 'Not a bad idea,' he admitted. The three of them, leaving the men with Scheki, made a quick reconnaissance of the ruined masonry Brandon had stumbled on. Under its covering of foliage it proved to be all that was left of some gigantic building, the floor plan of which must at one time have been a hundred yards square. Jagged remnants of wall rose to twenty feet in height in some places, and they came on traces of hard paved flooring as well.

'Quite a place,' said Mike wonderingly. 'I should have liked to have seen the people who lived here when it was a going concern.'

'I'm wondering if the jungle was so prolific then,' put in Litzgor. He prodded at the stonework with the tip of a machete.

'The point is academic,' said Brandon firmly. 'What we have to decide is where we shall make our camp.'

'What's wrong with settling down against that wall over there?' said Dorton. 'It looks as good as anywhere, and the scrub isn't quite so thick.'

Brandon agreed. Calling to Scheki, he gave orders for the making of camp. Soon the cooking fires were going and the men were busying themselves. They had had little chance during the day to grow restless, for Brandon and Scheki had kept them moving as fast as possible, and fatigue ensured that they did not discuss the earlier disasters among themselves.

Mindful of the treacherous attack that had been made on the previous night, Brandon set watches as soon as darkness fell. Litzgor took first spell when the remainder of the party turned in. Then Dorton relieved him. Brandon slept with his senses on the alert, and he knew that Scheki would be doing the same. The two of them had made too many safaris in the past not to know each other's capabilities.

Dorton exchanged a brief whispered

conversation with Jan Litzgor when the two changed places. Litzgor had nothing to report. The night was quiet. Too quiet, Brandon had thought earlier on. It struck him as uncanny when he suddenly realised that there were no birds in this place of ruined masonry from a different age. Somehow it reminded him forcibly of the strange unclassified reptiles which had attacked them yesterday.

Mike Dorton, too, was remembering the same sort of thing. He could not help admitting to himself that he was uneasy as he sat on the ground and cradled his rifle, his back resting comfortably against a *mchwili* tree.

His tour of duty was halfway through when the faintest sound reached his ears. Keyed up as he was, he stiffened and swung his rifle round to cover the section of darkness from which he thought it came. Again the whisper of noise caught his attention. But this time it seemed to come from somewhere else. The hair on the nape of his neck rose and prickled eerily, the chill of fear running down his spine. The camp was entirely surrounded, he told himself. But what was it surrounded by?

Getting to his knees, he crouched against the dark bole of the tree, partly concealed by the shadows beyond the edge if the fire-lit circle around the camp. Swinging his rifle round in an arc, he wondered if he ought to waken Brandon. But he was not even sure that he had actually heard anything, now he came to think about it. Was the ruined city or whatever it was haunted?

Then a sound that was really a sound reached his ears. A twig snapped with a crack like a pistol shot. Dorton gave a gasp and whirled round to the quarter of the new menace. As he did so he gave a shout, knowing that Brandon would waken in a moment. Hampered by the darkness, he searched for a target, but found nothing in the gloom. Then a sharp whisper of noise sent him flat on the ground, remembering the arrow that had ended a man's life on the previous night.

Sure enough, he heard the swoosh of something passing through the air. There was a thud as it struck the *mchwili* tree against which he had been resting. He fired in the approximate direction of the attack. Only the echoes came back to him, deep and reverberating in the green shrouded dark.

Rex Brandon and Litzgor came hurtling from their tents. Brandon called out for Scheki. The men were roused by the sudden commotion, and their startled cries completely drowned any noise there might have been to give them a line on Dorton's unseen foe.

Brandon flashed a powerful torch round. He ordered the men to be silent. Not a murmur of sound stirred in the hot night around them.

Dorton said: 'Someone shot at me with a bow, Rex. It must have been the same blighter who killed Irnpal last night!' He turned to the tree, searching for the arrow, hoping it would still be there.

'You were certainly shot at,' said Brandon grimly. He took a step closer to the tree, reaching up and wrenching a long-shafted arrow from where it was embedded in the wood.

'Wonder he didn't hit me!' grunted

Dorton disgustedly. 'I must have made a sitting target in the firelight!'

Brandon frowned and glanced hurriedly over his shoulder. Litzgor caught his eye and nodded.

'I wonder if they meant to get you, Mike,' said Brandon. 'You didn't notice this, I take it?'

'What?'

Brandon detached a slip of white paper from the shaft of the arrow. It was held in place by an elastic band. Dorton and Litzgor whistled in amazement. Brandon stripped the paper off and unrolled it while Mike held the flashlamp.

'Last night was a warning,' Brandon read aloud. 'You have lost one man. Tonight is a second warning. Unless you turn back, you will be wiped out completely. Take heed and beware of the ruined city, or it may be your grave.'

Dorton pulled his left ear in a fever of excitement. 'Written in English!' he gasped. 'Rex, what in the world's going on?'

Brandon handed the message to Litzgor. 'I wouldn't know,' he said quietly. 'But it's perfectly obvious that we're up against something more than hostile natives. Whether that was fired by the person who wrote it or not, we can't say, but its meaning is plain. We're not wanted in this neighbourhood!'

'No one is going to drive *me* out!' snapped Litzgor in a fierce whisper that was charged with hatred. 'The person who sent that warning must be the same white woman who led the natives against us before. She has my latest invention, and I mean to get it back if I die in the attempt!'

'We probably all shall,' said Dorton sourly. 'If you ask me, we're nothing but a bunch of idiots. This thing's getting beyond a joke. They're whittling us down, and when they're good and ready they'll wipe us out!'

Brandon grasped his wrist tightly. 'None of that!' he said, almost harshly. 'What are you trying to do, scare the life out of Scheki and the men? We'd look fools if they turned tail and fled, wouldn't we?'

'Sorry,' mumbled Dorton. 'I'm losing my grip. Don't take any notice of what I say, Rex.'

The three of them moved over and

joined Scheki where he was pacifying the frightened men. 'Tell them to go back to sleep,' said Brandon firmly. 'There's nothing to be afraid of, Scheki. We've received a warning, that's all.'

'I hope it is all, *bwana*,' murmured the headman gravely. 'These worthless fellows keep remembering that a few days ago they numbered seven. Now they are five, and they think they will soon be none.'

Brandon compressed his lips, but said nothing. Then: 'Keep a big fire going, Scheki,' he advised. 'It helps to give men courage. We shall not be attacked again tonight.'

He gave a nod. Brandon could see that he was scared, but his loyalty to his employer was greater than fear.

'You turn in now, Mike,' said Brandon. 'I'll take over from you. Scheki and I can share the watch for the rest of the night.'

Dorton started to protest, but the look in Brandon's eyes decided him to keep quiet. He merely nodded and walked across to his tent.

Nothing more happened during the

hours that preceded dawn. At breakfast the three of them held a council of war. It was unanimously agreed that they should push on and disregard the strange warning they had received during the night.

'If we watch our step we ought to be all right,' said Brandon. 'Mind you, I don't fancy the prospects much, but I'm damned if I'll throw in my hand without putting up a fight of some sort!'

'We are well armed,' pointed out Litzgor stoutly.

'I think we shall have to cut the baggage a little more,' Brandon said. 'There's not a lot we can dispense with, but if they don't have to carry so much, the men will feel less like jibbing in the face of danger.'

Brandon and Dorton took the lead, with the five men between themselves and a rearguard composed of Litzgor and Scheki. Every member of the party was armed, even the men carrying their spears as best they could with their loads.

It was when they had been pressing forward for a full hour that Dorton frowned and muttered. Brandon shot him a sidelong glance.

Dorton said: 'I've just remembered something.'

'Don't keep it a secret!'

Dorton grinned broadly. 'That warning mentioned a ruined city,' he mused. 'Was that where we camped last night, or did it refer to another place? We were told to beware of it, remember?'

Brandon considered. 'I think it was a figure of speech, Mike,' he answered. 'That ancient building was probably part of the city. The undergrowth was so dense that we only saw our own particular ruin.'

'Hmm . . . I still wonder.' Dorton fell silent again.

All that day they struggled on through the jungle, waging a constant war against insects, heat, undergrowth and the steepness of the slopes they were climbing. Never in his life had Brandon experienced such inhospitable country. Moving by compass, he kept as close to the mapped route of the Chargam River as possible. The day was well advanced when the ground suddenly levelled off without warning and they were no longer climbing.

'Think we've reached the top?' queried

Dorton. 'Phew! It's hot!'

Brandon halted, looking about curiously. There was a rank smell in the air, like rotting vegetation.

'No,' he said, slowly. 'I don't think we've reached the top, Mike. We're on the edge of a pocket of swamp land if you ask me. Feel the ground; it's soft underfoot.'

Dorton stamped his booted foot and brought up a faint squelching noise. 'You're right,' he said. 'What do we do?'

Litzgor came up and joined them. The men murmured uneasily among themselves until Scheki silenced them, waiting for a decision from Brandon.

Brandon said: 'We'd better carry straight on till we find out what the country's like. If this swamp gets any worse, we can always make a detour. It may be nothing.'

They nodded and started off again, content to leave the leadership in the hands of Brandon.

After a few minutes' progress, the density of scrub and moisture-laden thorn growth grew less and less. Long, dank jungle grass sprouted at their feet and clogged movement almost as much as the thorn had done previously. But they could see ahead for some distance, which they had not been able to do before. But, with evening drawing on, it was essential to find a suitable place to make camp. The softness of the ground did not reassure Brandon, but it was too late now to backtrack and select more solid ground.

Brandon and his companions were beginning to grow uneasy when they caught sight of the ruins ahead. Jagged stumps of stone thrust upwards through the thin undergrowth, marking the site of what must once have been a fair-sized town or city.

'The ruined city,' whispered Dorton. 'Surely it isn't built on a swamp, Rex? No one would do a crazy thing-like that!'

Brandon said nothing, but hurried on ahead with Dorton while the remainder followed at a distance.

Presently the mystery of the swamp-bound ruins became clear. The place had been built in the long-dead past on an island of solid rock amid a sea of inhospitable sogginess into which the feet of the men sank whenever they stood still for more than a minute. The smell of dank vegetation was heavy in the air, and even in its heyday the city must have been a curiously unpleasant place in which to live.

'We'll have to take what we find,' said Brandon. 'We'll camp here among the ruins for the night, Mike. I can't help about the warning we received. There's nothing else we can do under the circumstances.'

Choosing a square consisting of four-foot-high crumbling walls, the party spread out and made themselves as comfortable as possible. Big fires were lit, and the men prepared a meal. Since they did not know what the arrow-delivered warning had said, the very fact that they were surrounded by strong walls of stone gave them confidence. They were even able to joke among themselves when the distant roar of a lion broke the stillness of the jungle. Its bellow silenced every other whispering sound, freezing the tiny creatures of the night into immobility for minutes on end. Night settled down on the small safari party. Even Brandon found it strange to be camped on such an ancient site. He leant back against the nearest wall, his rifle across his knees, trying to picture what the original inhabitants of this dead city had been like; what their lives had consisted of; in what manner they had perished and left their city to decay.

Presently he gave up the puzzle and went to sleep. Taking the last watch himself, he selected a position to one side of the narrow entrance to their fort-like encampment. Everything seemed quiet, but Brandon was not fool enough to be lulled by the apparent peace.

He had been in position for a full hour before he became aware of some instinctive warning that other eyes were alive in the night. That odd sixth sense which had saved his life on many occasions in the past stirred within him.

The little camp was being watched. He knew it as surely as if he could see the actual watcher, but from what direction the possible threat might come he had as yet no idea. Tense in the fire-shot gloom, he waited, listening with every nerve in his tough, hard body alert and keyed up.

The feeling of being watched persisted, but he crushed the natural urge to wake the rest of the party. There would be little sense in doing so, and such a move might well hasten any attack that was in course of preparation.

Then the tiniest sound reached his ears from beyond the entrance to the ruin. Brandon did not remain where he was. Instead he crept out towards the source of the faint noise. Moving like a ghost, he slipped silently through the dense shadows for several yards, reaching a second wall in the tangle of ruins. Glancing back, he saw the reflected glare of the campfire rising from within the square enclosure of the camp. Then a dark and formless shape materialised just in front of him. A dry stick of wood cracked loudly, and someone suppressed a gasp of dismay at the sound.

Brandon froze where he was, watching through narrowed eyes as the shape of a figure came towards him. When it was so close that he could have reached out and touched it, he made a swift movement.

The figure stopped abruptly, hesitated, and turned to flee. Brandon's long arm whipped out and clamped on a wrist, fastening it tightly in a steely grip.

'Snooping?' he murmured softly. 'Let's have a look at you!'

# 5

'Far Enough, Stranger!'

The figure in Brandon's grasp gave a startled yelp. There was a brief but futile struggle which lasted for only a second or two, then Brandon was master of the situation. In the thick darkness he recognised the face and figure of his captive as belonging to a woman.

Even as the amazing fact penetrated his understanding, he was urging her back to the ruined walls of the campsite. Seen in the glow of the fire, she looked to be no more than twenty. Brandon had at first imagined that he had caught the mysterious woman who was reputed to lead attacks by some native tribe with a lion as her pet. But this woman was plainly not the one. It was clear at a glance that she was in a very dishevelled state and more than a little frightened by the situation in which she found herself. Mike Dorton and Jan Litzgor were wakened by the sound of Brandon's arrival, for he made no effort to keep it a secret now. The two men, as well as Scheki and the others, crowded round him curiously.

Brandon turned the woman so that the firelight played on her features. Under the lines of strain and fear that etched themselves on her face, she was attractive in a dark-haired, elfin fashion.

'Sit down,' said Brandon sternly. He kept her covered while Mike Dorton ran his hands over her clothes for any hidden weapon.

The woman made a weary gesture with her right hand. 'It's all right,' she said quietly. 'I'm not armed. I'm running away, if you really want to know. There's no need to act in this dramatic way. But now that I've arrived, I may as well tell you you're in frightful danger.'

Brandon stared at her hard, trying to assure himself that this was not a trick. The innate honesty of her features made him realise she was speaking the truth. He lowered his rifle and nodded to Litzgor and Dorton. 'Very well,' he said gently. 'We're friends. Now tell us what this is all about. What are you doing running around in a place like this at night? Where does the danger come in?'

She licked her lips nervously, glancing round at the faces of her captors — or friends. 'I knew you were camped here,' she said. 'I heard them talking and took a chance on slipping away. There's never been an opportunity till tonight.'

Brandon said: 'Wouldn't it be better if you began at the beginning? What's your name, for a start?'

'Charmaine Rickards,' she answered. 'It won't mean anything to you, I don't suppose . . . '

Brandon frowned. 'Rickards . . . ' he mused. 'Any relation to young Tom Rickards, the mining authority who was murdered about a year ago?'

The woman swallowed quickly. Then: 'Yes,' she whispered unhappily. 'He was my brother. He — ' The rest of her sentence was cut short by a sudden yell from the dark beyond the camp. At the same moment, a spear came whistling over the wall and thudded into the ground almost at Brandon's feet. He stared at it quivering there for an instant, then spun round and shouted orders. The yell from the darkness had been the signal for attack.

Almost before the men had time to grab their weapons, a screaming horde of half-seen natives hurled themselves in at the entrance to the ruin enclosure. Many others were climbing the shallow walls. Arrows and spears fell thick and fast as the small safari party took up defence positions and prepared to fight for their lives.

Brandon worked his rifle with deadly effect, pouring a hail of steel-jacketed bullets into the mass of men who were threatening to swamp them from the entrance. Mike Dorton and Litzgor were dealing with the enemy who scaled the wall. Scheki and his men, armed with spare rifles and shotguns, concentrated on destroying any of the invaders who succeeded in entering the enclosure. The din was indescribable, for not only were the attackers yelling their heads off, but Brandon's men also gave vent to their feelings in an audible fashion. And on top of all the vocal noise, the air was hideous with the crackle and roar of the gunfire.

Brandon, close to one of the walls, found the woman at his side. 'Give me your revolver,' she said urgently. He grinned and unhooked it from his belt, then continued firing with all the coolness he could muster. Deep in his heart he knew that the party was up against something too big to be sanguine about. There seemed to be hundreds of the attacking natives, and it would only be a matter of time before they were overrun and wiped out. But he said nothing beyond a word of encouragement to the fugitive woman as she started firing with unexpected accuracy at the waves of yelling men.

Suddenly one of the men gave a cry of agony and threw up his arms, pitching forward almost face down into the embers of the fire. He lay quite still, a long-shafted spear protruding from between his shoulder blades.

Brandon's mouth tightened grimly. This was only the first casualty. If there were many more, the game would be up, especially if any of the whites were struck down.

Charmaine was using her revolver steadily. Dorton and Litzgor proved themselves well able to attend to their part of the fight. Brandon glanced anxiously at the sky. The long night was drawing to a close. Already there was a greyness in the east which heralded the rising of the sun. What would happen with daylight? he wondered. They would then be more vulnerable than ever, for there would not even be darkness to afford them cover.

'Keep 'em off!' shouted Dorton. 'They're thinning out now! We've got them beat if we keep it up.'

But within the next few minutes, Dorton himself was hit by a spear. It pierced the fleshy part of his upper arm, and although the wound was not a serious one, it hampered the use of a rifle. Then three more of the men went down, badly hit.

Brandon looked about desperately. Things were growing unpleasant. The party was now reduced to Dorton, Litzgor, Scheki, Tooma, the last of the men, Charmaine, and himself. True, they had plenty of ammunition and enough rifles and guns to go round, but the odds were tremendous.

An enormous figure hurled himself in at the narrow entrance of the camp, brandishing a spear above his head. He made a dead set at reaching Brandon. Brandon aimed and fired, but his rifle magazine was empty. He gave a yell and rose to his feet, clubbing his rifle. From the corner of his eye he saw that others of the attacking natives were making determined efforts to get inside the enclosure and finish off the battle. The butt of the rifle crashed on the man's skull with a sickening crunch of bone. At the same instant, Charmaine killed another of the enemy as the man tried to follow Brandon's intending killer. Then Brandon was slipping in a fresh clip of ammunition with frantic haste. A second wave of men launched themselves. It was as if they were intent on getting the party before daylight broke.

Backs to the wall with a vengeance, the little party gave as good as they received. The assaulting natives were dropping on all sides. Minor wounds were inflicted on Litzgor and Brandon. Then Tooma fell, speared to death. Only Charmaine escaped unscathed. But the whites were weakening. The continued strain of fighting such odds was beginning to tell on them. Nor did their wounds help the situation.

Scheki clubbed his empty rifle when the magazine ran out and he was too badly pressed to reload. Flailing out to right and left, he felled half a dozen of the natives, but was himself struck down by a well-aimed throwing club.

Brandon knew the end was close. Their attackers seemed to be coming from all sides now. They clambered over the shallow walls in waves of yelling fury as the first flush of dawn lightened the sky and dispelled the shadows of night.

Charmaine, reloading Brandon's revolver feverishly, gave a gasp of dismay as she saw what was going to happen. 'They'll finish us next time!' she whispered fearfully.

'Keep your chin up,' said Brandon, pumping bullets into the tightly packed mass of natives who were pressing in through the entrance.

'Give 'em hell!' roared Dorton. He fired from the hip, his wounded arm making it almost impossible for him to use a rifle at the shoulder. One of the foremost attackers went down screaming, hands clasped across his belly.

'Never do it!' gasped Litzgor desperately. 'They've got us where they want us now! This is the end!'

A fresh assault force swept in through the entrance and came in over the walls. For long seconds Brandon saw nothing but the whirling faces of the enemy, hearing their stamping feet and seeing writhing bodies as they weaved in and out before making the final attack. Determined to sell his life as dearly as he could, he shouted to the others to be ready for a charge. There was just the slimmest chance that they might be able to break out if they killed as they went and carved a path to freedom. But he knew it was a forlorn hope. However, anything was better than waiting for death.

'Ready?' shouted Brandon. 'Rush 'em!' He led the charge himself, glad to see that the rest of the party were close behind him and spreading out on either side, firing and clubbing for all they were worth. Even Scheki, who had by this time recovered his senses, was doing his bit. Charmaine, frightened though she was, stayed close to Brandon, using her revolver with an efficiency that was worth two badly used guns.

They were right in the centre of a milling horde of natives by this time, fighting their way through inch by inch, lashing out on both sides when their guns were empty. But the pace was slowed down. They were barely moving forward towards the entrance now. Hemmed in on all sides, it looked as if their desperate bid for freedom was doomed.

Turning so that they fought in the form of a tight square, the little party fended off the weight of numbers launched against them. Brandon was hit by a club, but managed to duck and escape the full force of the blow. Then Charmaine stopped firing and toppled over sideways, knocked senseless by a glancing club blow.

Brandon cursed and stood guard over her, whirling his heavy rifle round his head and bringing down anyone who dared to approach. Spears sang past his head; an arrow plucked at the sleeve of his bush shirt.

Dorton, panting for breath, crammed some shells into his revolver and killed three of his nearest attackers. 'It's no good!' he gasped. 'We can't get away with it, Rex. This is goodbye, I'm afraid!'

Brandon said nothing. He prepared to kill as many of the natives as he could before going down himself. Charmaine stirred uneasily at his feet. Litzgor groaned as the blade of a spear lanced his flesh. Scheki, bleeding from a dozen minor wounds, yelled encouragement to the others as he flung himself forward, cutting and hacking a few yards nearer the enclosure entrance.

Then, without any warning, the pressure of weapons around them slackened; the sting seemed to go from the heart of the attack. In the background Brandon heard an urgent shouting. He could not understand what was said, but a moment later most of the natives began to retreat, withdrawing hurriedly to a point outside the enclosure.

'What's bitten them now?' demanded Dorton grimly. 'It looks as if someone's called them off. This is crazy!'

'Never mind that!' snapped Brandon. 'Let's get out of here while the going's good!' He handed his rifle to Scheki, then quickly bent and picked up Charmaine. At a run they left the enclosure, following on the heels of the last of the native attackers.

Not until they were outside and breaking a way through the scrub in the opposite direction to that taken by the men did they realise the cause of the hurried withdrawal of their enemy. Unexpectedly in the grey light of dawn came the long and ferocious bellow of an angry lion. A wail of fear escaped from the last of the attackers. Scheki looked at Brandon with something like dismay, wondering whether his employer was in a fit state to tackle a lion at this stage. Brandon bared his teeth in a grin as he led the way through the scrub, still carrying Charmaine.

Dorton and Litzgor brought up the rear. It was Dorton who saw what was happening when they paused a hundred yards from the ruined enclosure.

'Good God, Rex!' he exclaimed. 'The devils have been attacked by another tribe by the look of it!' Brandon lowered Charmaine to the ground and stared in the direction Dorton was pointing. Sure enough, he saw the men who had tried so hard to kill them engaged in a life-and-death battle with others of their kind. But it was not only against another tribe of men that they were fighting. The great tawny shape of a jungle lion sprang this way and that as it hurled itself against the enemy.

Litzgor sucked in his breath. 'The lion!' he muttered. 'It can't be!'

'What?' demanded Brandon. He felt weak after the long battle in the enclosure. Then he realised what Litzgor was referring to. Straining his eyes in the early light of day, he saw what he half-expected to.

Hovering on the fringe of the battle, in which fully a hundred men were locked in mortal combat, was the figure of a tall white woman. Her voice reached his ears, high and shrill as she encouraged her own men and the lion.

In a few seconds the outcome of the fight was no longer in doubt. The native lion put renewed fear into the men who had attacked Brandon's party. Already exhausted by the fight in the enclosure, they fell easy prey to the combined strength of the newcomers. Even as Brandon and his friends watched, they broke and fled in confusion.

Brandon wasted no more time. A glance at Charmaine's face showed him that she had recovered her senses and was struggling to a sitting position, shaking her head and passing a hand across her forehead.

'Come on!' he said urgently. 'This is no place for us. Once that woman's outfit overcomes the others, they'll be after us. This is your virago with the lion, I take it, Mike?'

Dorton nodded quickly. 'That's the female!' he said in a tone of respect. 'She's no friend of mine. Let's be moving before they see us!'

Suiting action to their words, the whole party started off through the scrub, heading as fast as they could for thicker cover. Charmaine, when she caught a glimpse of the white woman and heard the ferocious roars of the man-killer lion, turned pale and suddenly clung to Brandon's arm. 'Don't let her get me again!' she begged in a voice that was close to panic.

Brandon glanced down at her sympathetically. 'Don't worry,' he said. 'If she gets you, she'll have to get us all, and that won't happen in a hurry if we keep our heads.'

They forced a way through dense undergrowth. The din of the pitched battle going on in their rear was still loud enough to drown most of the noise they made, but Brandon knew there was little time to waste. If they were once seen and chased, they would stand no chance of escaping death or capture. The fact that they were up against the mysterious white woman and her lion was something else that spurred Brandon into making a bid for freedom. He wanted to solve this mystery if he could, and being killed in a jungle battle was no way to do it.

The sounds of battle faded out behind them. They were struggling through dense jungle country now. There were traces of ruined buildings all round them, but Brandon and his companions had had enough of ruins for a while. There seemed to be too much peril in these ancient remains.

'What's the plan?' demanded Litzgor.

'We'll find a spot to lie up and collect ourselves first of all,' answered Brandon. 'That's our best plan.'

'Lead on, Rex!' said Dorton. 'We're all with you.'

They started off again, reaching a small clearing in the undergrowth. The clearing had once been the floor of some vast building, for it was paved with giant slabs of stone which had kept the foliage down.

Brandon paused, looking round for some suitable place of concealment. The sounds of the distant battle had faded out altogether by this time. Sweating and almost at the end of their tether, the whites and Scheki staggered across the little clearing to the dense wall of undergrowth on the far side.

Forcing their way through, they came at last to a solid wall of masonry which brought them to a sudden halt. Brandon turned and mopped his brow. 'This'll do for the time being,' he grunted wearily.

They stared about, taking in the narrow confines of the scene: a stone wall of ancient rock in front of them; the green banks of the jungle undergrowth pressing in their rear. Without another word they sank to the ground, tired and exhausted from the strain of the last hectic hour.

Brandon closed his eyes. They were still closed when Charmaine Rickards gave a gasp of dismay and shook him violently by the shoulder. Fully awake in an instant, Brandon sat up with a jerk, his gun in his hand. But he was too late.

Grinning down at them, and covering them with two heavy automatic pistols, was a man, short and thick in stature, ugly of countenance.

Before Brandon could speak or make a move, the man said: 'I guess this is far enough, stranger! Now you best put your hands up and take it easy!'

# 6

## Dwellers of the Underground

Sick at heart, Brandon stared back at the evil face of the ragged-looking white man.

'Nothing you can do about it, brother,' drawled the man in a nasal voice. 'You sure are in trouble, but it may work out right if you act sensible.'

'Who are you?' demanded Jan Litzgor uneasily. He was sneaking his hand down to lift his revolver. The man saw the movement, stealthy though it was.

'I wouldn't do that,' he advised grimly. 'Unless you want to die right here and now, of course.'

'What's the idea?' grunted Dorton, glancing at Litzgor.

The man jerked his two automatics. 'The idea, my young friend, is that you're my prisoners. We're going places!'

Brandon was on the point of saying

something caustic when Charmaine cut him short.

'I hoped I'd seen the last of you, Raoul!' she said in a tone full of bitterness. 'Why do you hound me like this?'

'Shut up!' the man told her curtly. 'There'll be trouble for you if you've shot your mouth off to this bunch of saps!'

'All right!' said Brandon harshly. 'We're your prisoners. There is no need to threaten us or insult our mentality. What do you want with us?'

The man grinned unpleasantly. 'I just don't like any strangers around,' he answered. 'Get up, the lot of you! Now march!'

Brandon had been waiting for that. Once they were on the move in the undergrowth, he thought there might be a chance of making a break. But here again his hopes were dashed. No sooner had they climbed to their feet than half a dozen men appeared from the scrub. They were tall and well developed, merciless-looking and fully armed. The man with the automatics spoke to them in some local dialect which Brandon did not understand. The meaning of his words was, however, plain, for the natives crowded round and encircled the whites.

'Long walk,' said their captor cheerfully. 'Get moving and make it snappy. Charmaine, honey, you better stick with me!' He laughed as the woman shrank even closer to Brandon. Then: 'O.K., kid, have it your own way! My time'll come later — when you tell us what we want to know.'

Charmaine glared at him balefully. 'You'll never make me talk!' she retorted fiercely.

'Maybe Connie'll think up a way,' was the answer. The tone in which it was said gave Brandon some inkling of the man they were up against. For the most part he did not fully comprehend the gist of the conversation between the man and Charmaine Rickards, but it was obvious now that she had escaped from him. He could only think that the person called Connie must be the mysterious woman with the lion. It was an interesting supposition.

Led by their captor and hemmed in and disarmed by the natives, the party started off along a narrow jungle path in the undergrowth. They travelled for what seemed a considerable time. The sun rose and increased in heat till Brandon longed for a cool drink. He realised that none of them had eaten anything since the previous evening, and apart from being exhausted from the battle they had fought they were also hungry and thirsty.

It must have been mid-day before they halted. The man whose name was Raoul came to a stop after climbing a steep rise in the ground. He stopped because there was a sheer drop of well over a hundred feet immediately in front of him. The escorting men brought their prisoners to a standstill in his rear. Raoul turned and grinned vindictively.

'Remember this, don't you, Charmaine?' he murmured.

The woman stood close beside Brandon. Her arm touched his and he felt her shudder. She said nothing in reply.

Raoul turned again and edged along the side of the ravine. Brandon could now see that it was fifty yards or thereabouts in width, and that on the opposite side was a rocky platform with more of the ruined buildings and jagged lumps of masonry. They were closed in behind by thick banks of vegetation. Crossing the ravine some yards further along the edge was a narrow bridge consisting of a single span of rock. Raoul was making towards it. The bridge was narrow and its surface so uneven that in parts it was little more than a treacherous knife-edge.

Raoul stopped once again, gesturing to the bridge. 'Are we expected to walk across *that*?' demanded Dorton.

Raoul grinned. 'You'll be safe enough,' he said. 'I do it often. Charmaine's done it more than once, too. Ask her if it's safe!'

Dorton glanced at her, but she was staring at Raoul with fear and dislike in her eyes.

'Well, get on with it!' said Litzgor. 'If we're going across, we may as well go!'

Raoul ignored the remark. Walking in single file, the party crossed the bridge. Even Brandon did not like the look of the drop below them, but the stone bridge itself was firm enough.

Reaching the opposite side of the ravine they halted again, covered by Raoul and surrounded by the six tall men. 'For the benefit of strangers,' said Raoul in a patronising tone, 'you are now standing on a natural stronghold. The bridge we just crossed is the only means of access to it.'

'Gee, you don't say!' drawled Dorton, mimicking the man's nasal voice. 'What do you do in a place like this? Keep chickens or something?'

Raoul scowled. 'You'll learn,' he snapped. 'March!'

The whole party started off towards the nearest of the ancient ruins. Brandon found time to marvel at a people who must once have existed here, wondering about them.

Raoul led the way to the largest pile of crumbling stone. It proved to be the decaying walls which surrounded a sort of overgrown courtyard. At the far end was a dark entrance. Raoul stopped when he reached it, speaking to the warriors in an undertone. Then he stared back the way they had come as if expecting to see something. Brandon turned his head and followed his gaze. What he saw brought a silent whistle to his lips.

Crossing the bridge at the head of a long file of men was the white woman he had seen when they escaped from the campsite. Close at her heels followed one of the biggest and most native-looking lions he had ever come across in the whole of his big-game hunting career. From that distance the great beast seemed tame enough, but Brandon remembered seeing it in the thick of the fight and remembered, too, that it had killed several of the rival tribesmen.

Charmaine, at his side, gave a gasp as she saw the retinue making its way towards them.

Raoul smirked, seeing her expression. 'Scared, honey?' he said, sneering. 'Connie won't hurt you — if you're good!'

Charmaine said nothing, but her eyes suddenly sought those of Brandon. There was an appealing look of trust in her glance. He wondered what story lay behind the situation into which he and his friends had been pitchforked. It was obviously one she found frightening. What was her relationship to these two lawless people of the wilds? he asked himself. There had been no opportunity to get her tale.

They stood there waiting. As the woman called Connie approached, Brandon took stock of her. She was a handsome creature with long, dark hair and a purposeful face. Her figure was powerful, but strictly feminine. Just as Litzgor and Mike Dorton had told him, she wore a leopard-skin bodice with bush breeches below. She wore no hat, but carried a rifle slung across her right shoulder and an automatic pistol in her belt. Her eyes, when she surveyed the prisoners, were cold and imperious. Yet there was passion in the lines of her face and the lift of her brow. Her mouth was wide and generous.

'So you got them after all, *cheri*?' she murmured in a soft voice.

Raoul grinned. 'Sure I did!' he answered. 'When I go after something I usually get it!'

The woman smiled thinly. 'Yes,' she said quietly. Then: 'Put them below,

Raoul. We'll discuss their future in a little while. The old man interests me because he's been in the district before. We just missed him, remember? But he dropped something when he got away.' She broke off. Her dark eyes came to rest on Charmaine. 'And you, my dear, will you be sensible now, or must we imprison you with the rest while we make up our minds as to which is the best way to loosen your tongue?'

Charmaine threw her head back. 'You won't make me talk!' she retorted firmly. 'Do what you like!'

Connie nodded thoughtfully. 'Just as I expected,' she said, glancing at the man. 'Get them below!'

Raoul nodded, then jerked his head at several of the natives who were waiting in silence nearby.

The great lion gave a rumbling growl. Connie snapped something to it so that it sank on its haunches at her side, nuzzling her hand. The men watched it fearfully. Even Brandon and his friends kept a wary eye on the enormous killer. Scheki, never very far from Brandon, looked frightened as well. Then they were all herded in through the darkly shadowed entrance at which Raoul had come to a stop.

A broad flight of stone steps, smooth and treacherous with age, led downwards into what seemed like the bowels of the earth. A flaming torch was held aloft by one of the natives to light the way. There were other torches fixed to the walls below ground. Some were already alight, others were touched in passing. Thin smoke and the yellow glare of flame added an uncanny atmosphere to the world into which the prisoners were being taken.

With Raoul in the lead, they covered what seemed to Brandon hundreds of yards of high-roofed passageways which turned and doubled back on themselves time after time. They passed a number of ancient wooden doors set in the walls of the passages, and it seemed to Brandon that these places must have been the endless cellars of the great buildings which had once stood above the ground.

Though no one mentioned it, they were all glad to see that the woman, Connie, and her lion had remained aboveground;

or, if they had followed the party down through the entrance, the two of them had taken another route.

Raoul at length stopped outside a door, the framework of which had been reinforced with stout new timber. There was also a modern lock set in it, and it had every appearance of having been prepared especially as a prison cell.

'This is where they kept me before,' whispered Charmaine a little breathlessly. 'I'll tell you all about it when we have a chance to talk. You've been wonderful, and I'm sorry I landed you in trouble.'

'Wasn't your fault,' murmured Brandon. 'We were heading for it anyway, as far as I can see.'

Raoul caught the murmur of their voices and scowled, but said nothing. He took a key from his pocket and unlocked the door, flinging it wide and standing back. 'In you go!' he said harshly. 'And think yourselves mighty lucky that Connie didn't say you should be shot out of hand!'

'You're very considerate for our health,' said Brandon in a quietly taunting fashion.

Raoul snarled something as Brandon went past him through the door. The others followed close on his heels, then the door was slammed shut behind them and they turned to look at one another in something like dismay. Seen in the uncertain light of a flickering torch that was set in a holder against the wall, their faces were haggard and their clothing dishevelled in the extreme.

Brandon shrugged, his mouth set in a firm, hard line. He glanced round at the walls of their cell. It was fairly spacious, and the cool of the stone walls was welcome enough. But it would prove an impossible place from which to escape. He realised that at a glance. Not a chink showed between the great slabs of stone from which the walls were fashioned, and the roof was high and out of reach. The floor, like the walls, was paved in stone. And the inside of the heavy door had every appearance of being as solid as the rock of the walls.

'I suggest we take a well-earned rest,' he said with a cheerful grin. 'There's nothing we can do at the moment.'

Dorton sank to the ground, his back against the wall. It was cool and restful to the touch. He let his chin sink to his chest and closed his eyes. The slight wound in his arm was setting up a throb that troubled him.

Brandon sat down with a sigh of relief. He looked up at Charmaine and gave her a smile. 'Sit down,' he advised. 'I don't want to press you, Miss Rickards, but I must admit that I'm consumed by curiosity as to how you got yourself entangled with these strange people. What are they?'

She passed a weary hand across her face, then sat on the floor beside him. Scheki stretched himself out flat, eyes shut and breathing deep and relaxed. Jan Litzgor glanced at his companions, then began to pace the floor of the cell with deliberate and infuriating steps.

'I owe you an apology,' Charmaine began. 'I should not have drawn you into this. It wasn't your affair, and if I hadn't tried to sneak into your camp last night they might not have bothered to capture you.'

Litzgor paused in his striding up and down. 'Oh yes they would,' he stated firmly. 'You may not know it, Miss Rickards, but I and Mike there have almost fallen into their clutches before! And what's more, I lost the most precious thing I possessed. That appalling woman with the lion has it. Luckily, I doubt if she understands what it's for.'

'He's an inventor,' put in Dorton in a tired voice. 'We were attacked by the lovely Connie and her natives — to say nothing of the lion — and only got away by the skin of our teeth. That was a long time ago; you might not have been here then, of course.'

'But we didn't see this fellow, Raoul,' added Litzgor. 'He's a new one on me.'

'He's a murderer,' said Charmaine quietly.

Brandon raised his eyebrows slightly. 'Tell me,' he said.

She bit her lower lip. Then: 'My brother, as I told you, was Tom Rickards. He was murdered about a year ago, but they never caught the killer. Nor did they trace the woman my brother had married. There was a bit of scandal about the whole affair, but it didn't all get into the papers. This woman Connie is my sister-in-law. And Raoul is the man who killed Tom. As far as I can make out, Raoul is a deserter from the war days. He's an American by birth, but I don't think anyone would own him. As for Connie, I firmly believe she used him simply and solely as a means of doing away with Tom for her own ends.'

'Tom was a mining expert, wasn't he?' mused Brandon. 'Has that got anything to do with it?'

She frowned. 'I think it might have had,' she said. 'Tom was a gold expert, you know. So am I, to a much more limited degree. That's why they haven't killed me, of course. I can help them.'

'How?' It was Dorton who put the question.

'Let me explain,' she continued. 'I discovered a clue which put me on to Raoul as Tom's killer. By then he had disappeared, and so had Connie. I remembered something Tom had said when they were both in earshot — something meant for my ears alone. It was a wild guess, naturally, but I got a small safari together and trekked up here. This is the district Tom mentioned in the conversation I spoke of. You see, there's supposed to be one of the richest veins of virgin gold in the world up here.' She paused, looking round at the faces of her companions.

Litzgor drew a sharp breath. Dorton whistled softly. Brandon nodded, and Scheki remained silent.

'So you followed a hunch and guessed that they must have overheard your brother giving you the location?' Brandon mused. 'He was then murdered, and the pair of them came here with the object of finding the gold reef. Am I right?'

She nodded unhappily. 'They didn't count me,' she said. 'But when I stumbled on them together in the mountains and said I knew who'd murdered Tom, it was a different matter. They grabbed me. Their natives slaughtered my bearers, and then they tried to make me tell them where the gold vein lies. As a matter of fact, I couldn't have done so exactly if I'd been willing to. Tom only gave me vague direction — after all, he'd only been here once. We were going to check it ourselves, you see. But anyway, I flatly refused to discuss the matter with Connie and Raoul. They tried being rough; they tried starving me; keeping me without water; and other things. It was when they threatened to turn me over to the natives for a few hours that I really got scared. And that was when a chance to run away came along. I took it, and you know the rest.' She stopped and drew a deep breath.

'My God, what a pair of devils!' muttered Mike Dorton. Brandon nodded grimly.

But it was Litzgor who sprung the greatest surprise of all. 'This gold reef,' he began. 'I could find it.'

'You know where it lies?' queried Brandon, puzzled.

Litzgor shook his head. 'No,' he admitted. 'But my invention — the thing that woman stole — is an electronic device for locating gold-bearing ore. Dorton and I were up here to test it out under rigorous conditions when we ran across these people and almost lost our lives, to say nothing of my invention.'

'I see,' said Brandon quietly. 'But they can't have realised the value of their loot or they'd have dispensed with Miss Rickards by the most direct means. All the time she's alive, she's a potential danger to them. With her dead, they wouldn't have to worry.'

Dorton scratched his head. 'In that case,' he said quietly, 'they must under no circumstances discover what Jan's invention is for. If they do, it will be signing her death warrant.'

Litzgor grunted and nodded quickly. 'You're right!' he agreed. 'They'll get nothing out of me, I can promise you.'

Brandon was not so sure. He had an idea that the man Raoul would be capable of getting information out of anyone if he was given a free hand. But he kept his doubts to himself.

A few moments later the key turned in the lock of the door and Connie stood looking in at them. Close at her side was the enormous lion, growling softly when it saw the prisoners.

'Greetings!' she said. 'I brought Leo with me for protection.'

Brandon met her gaze coldly. 'What do you want?' he asked.

'A chat with your funny little friend who left us with an odd sort of gadget when he fled from Leo last time,' she replied with a smile. 'Come, Mr. Litzgor. There is no reason why we should be enemies.'

After a moment's agonised silence, Jan Litzgor followed Connie from the cell, leaving the others gravely troubled.

# 7

## 'Run For Your Life!'

No sooner had the door closed on Connie and her fearsome escort than Brandon sprung towards it. He was moving before the rest of the party had time to draw breath or discuss this latest disaster.

In the face of the killer lion, even Brandon had hesitated to launch an attack on Connie to prevent her taking Litzgor. But it was not only the presence of the ferocious beast that had deterred him. He guessed that if she did not return to Raoul with the prisoner, a search would be made, and then they could not expect mercy. But at the same time, he could not afford to let them work on Litzgor for long. There were ways of making a man divulge his secrets, however strong his will might be.

'You'll never get that open, Rex,' said Mike with a sort of groan. 'Now they've got Jan to themselves, anything can happen.' He looked across at Charmaine. Her face was pale and drawn. She met his eyes and bit her lower lip in a worried fashion.

Brandon said nothing for a moment. He gripped the door handle and turned it quickly, pulling towards him as he did so. There was no movement. He dipped to one knee and examined the door lock closely.

'What do you expect to do?' queried Dorton. 'That's as solid as a rock, man!'

Brandon glanced up. There was a faint grin on his face. 'Not quite, Mike,' he replied. 'I've got very keen ears. Didn't you notice anything odd when she shut the door?'

Dorton frowned. Charmaine made a gesture. Scheki went towards Brandon.

'I hear, too, *bwana*,' he said. 'It was not a proper shutting, yebbo?'

Brandon nodded. 'The door shut all right,' he said. 'But the lock didn't shoot right home, I'm positive.' He broke off, frowning as he studied the thin slit. 'If I had a knife, I think I could do something with it,' he added slowly.

'Would this be any good?' said Charmaine eagerly. From inside her shirt she brought out a very small sheath knife. Rex eyed her wonderingly for a moment.

'How the dickens did you manage that?' he demanded with a grin of pleasure.

'They missed it when they caught us,' she explained. 'I just kept quiet about it in case of emergency.'

'Good for you!' exclaimed Mike.

Brandon went to work with the little knife, blessing the ingenuity of the woman. Just as he had hoped and prayed, the haft of the lock had not fully engaged in its socket. By the most careful manipulation, he was able to slip the point of the knife in behind the lock tongue and ease it back. The tip of the knife blade snapped off and brought a curse to his lips, but by then there was sufficient room to use the thicker part of the blade.

With a decisive click that was loud in the breathless silence of their prison cell, the lock snapped back and Brandon sighed his relief.

'Quiet, everyone!' he whispered. 'We've

got to take this carefully, remember. There may be guards in the passages.'

Charmaine's fingers pressed his arm in her excitement. Then Brandon was cautiously opening the door and peering out. A flaming torch illuminated the gloom outside. All the way along the subterranean passages were torches, the smell of their fumes acrid in the nostrils of the escaping party.

Moving in single file, with Brandon in the lead, the four of them started off in the direction from which they had been brought. It was as much by luck as judgment that Brandon picked the right route, for they soon discovered that the place was a veritable warren. When they paused at various intersections, they could hear the sounds of human voices from a distance. It became plain that part of the passages and the cellars opening off them were used as habitations, probably by the warriors who seemed to owe some allegiance to Connie and Raoul.

Eventually a square of daylight showed ahead. Brandon slowed down the pace, edging forward with the utmost caution.

The square of light proved to be a different entrance to the underground passages they had used before, but it looked out on the same section of ground. Charmaine gave a gasp as they took in the scene.

The end of the passage came out amid a tumble of ruins. By flattening themselves to the ground, they could watch without being seen; but the scene was not a pretty one. Below them lay a sort of shallow arena. Standing with their backs to the unseen watchers were a large group of the natives, their bodies liberally daubed with war paint. Brandon estimated the number to be fifty or sixty. They found a cleared space against a leaning chunk of masonry. In front of the stonework was Litzgor, his hands tied behind his back. On one side of him was Raoul; on the other Connie and her snarling lion. She rested one hand on its mane and stroked the thick hair unconcernedly.

Just in front of Litzgor, a native was bending over a fire. As Brandon and the others stared in fascination, he pulled a red-hot spear from the flames and waved it in the air.

'This is appalling!' breathed Charmaine. 'Can't we do something, Rex?' She shuddered as the full meaning of the scene penetrated her understanding. Litzgor stood with his chest bared, his body forced back against the stonework. From his drawn face, it was obvious that he knew what was coming.

Brandon's jaw hardened. 'Torture!' he muttered grimly. 'They're the worst pair of swine I've ever crossed. Wait here and don't make a sound!' He started easing himself up, ready to sprint for cover. 'When the fuss begins, take your chance and make a break, understand?'

Dorton nodded. 'Good luck,' he whispered. Brandon ghosted away, working through the ruins till he judged that he was somewhere behind the lump of stonework in front of which Litzgor was standing.

As if to confirm this, there was suddenly a thin, high scream. It echoed and was repeated. Immediately on its heels came a great shout from the assembled natives. Connie's lion roared defiantly.

Brandon bit his lip and worked inwards

as quickly as he could. Reaching the back of the lump of masonry, he started to climb it. The task was a simple one, for the stones were uneven and offered innumerable holds. Sprawled across the top, he peered over and down. Jan Litzgor, gripped firmly by Raoul and another of the natives, was sagging at the knees. The giant warrior with the red-hot spear was plunging the blade into the fire to reheat it. Connie smiled faintly as she studied the burn on Litzgor's chest.

'Next time it will be deeper,' she said. Her voice was almost a caress. 'You'll be only too glad to talk in a little while. Then we shall know how to work this gadget of yours!'

Litzgor threw his head back and spat something between his teeth. The woman flushed deeply. Raoul struck Litzgor across the mouth.

Brandon decided it was time to take a hand. From where he lay, he was partly concealed, and the eyes of the entire gathering were fixed on the torture scene. Feeling round, he found a large stone that was loose to the touch. He gave it a jerk and tested its weight, finding it almost too heavy to lift. Any other man but Brandon would have doubted his strength to hurl it; but Brandon had been in many tight spots in his life before and knew his capabilities.

The warrior with the red-hot spear came away from the fire and advanced on Litzgor. Litzgor was shaking where he stood, living through the hell of searing flesh before he felt the glowing tip of the spear.

In one single movement, Brandon was on his feet, the great chunk of stone gripped in both hands. He raised it above his head, then hurled it forwards, straight at the man with the torture weapon. The stone struck him on the forehead, smashing his skull and face to an unrecognisable pulp as he dropped to the ground. Instantly there was chaos below. The natives yelled their dismay, pressing forward to gather round their fallen comrade.

Brandon yelled to Litzgor, causing the startled man to turn his head upwards. 'Run for your life!' he shouted urgently.

'Go on, man. Run!' At the same time, Raoul secured a firmer hold on the prisoner. Connie looked up and caught sight of Brandon. Brandon seized another stone and hurled it down on top of Raoul, striking his shoulder. He cried out and let go of Litzgor, who sprang away and darted round the edge of the stonework.

Connie shouted something to her lion, but probably because of the general confusion the beast was slow in obeying. By the time it streaked off after Litzgor, the unfortunate man had reached the cover of the jungle and was lost to view.

Brandon, without waiting to argue with anyone, dropped on the far side of the stonework and raced after Litzgor. As he ran, he saw from the corner of his eye that the figures of Dorton, Charmaine and Scheki were moving swiftly through the undergrowth to intercept himself and the inventor.

The drumming sound of running feet in his rear made him look over his shoulder, to see the lion bounding after him with a horde of natives some distance further back. There was no sign of Connie or Raoul. It looked to Brandon as if the lion would overtake him. He gritted his teeth and raced on. Then he caught the sound of a horn being blown from way behind the natives. Another glance over his shoulder showed the lion halted in its tracks. The horn note was repeated and the animal turned, loping back towards the ruins.

Brandon, though relieved, was puzzled. He decided that Connie did not intend the lion to tear the escaping prisoners to pieces if she could help it. The natives, on the other hand, were out to recapture them. Plunging into the jungle close on the heels of Litzgor, he raced up beside the man, grabbing his arm and steering him towards a spot where he thought the rest of the party would converge.

Within a few seconds they were all together again. But the warriors were after them. 'Scatter!' snapped Brandon tersely. 'Make your way to the bridge. If we can cross it, we can hold them off.'

Without a word of protest they separated, running in various directions. Brandon set off in an arc which he hoped would bring him to the bridge across the ravine. If he could reach it and hold it, the way would be clear for his friends. Unarmed as they were, they faced danger with every step they took. Listening carefully, he grinned as he realised that the scattering movement of the party had thrown the natives off the scent. With five different lines to follow, they were now uncertain.

Moving as cautiously as he could, he finally arrived at the edge of the ravine some fifty yards from the point at which it was spanned by the narrow rock bridge. And there he halted, rooted to the spot by what he saw.

The bridge was no longer empty. Instead of giving a clear route to freedom, it was at the moment dominated by an enormous figure. Standing right in the middle of the span, shaggy head thrust forward and long arms hanging slack on each side of its body, was one of the biggest gorillas Brandon had seen in his life.

He touched his lips with the tip of his tongue, realising that before they could escape from the island of rock the great beast must be killed or driven off. Behind him he could hear the confused shouting of the natives as they combed the scrub for the fugitives. In the distance, too, his ears picked out the deep-throated bellow of the lion. By the sound of it, the creature had been briefed by its owner and was coming nearer to the bridge.

Filled with dismay at the situation which faced him, Brandon decided there was nothing for it but to make an attempt to dislodge the gorilla from its place on the bridge. It was not a task he fancied. Advancing on the bridge, he hurled a sharp-edged piece of stone at the massive ape. Struck on the chest, the beast gave a roar of defiance and raised its arm. But it did not retreat as he had hoped it would. Instead it came towards his end of the bridge.

Brandon prepared to meet it. This would not be the first time he had fought a gorilla bare-handed, but he realised he was tired and close to being exhausted. The prospects were none too bright.

Halting at the end of the bridge, the giant ape roared again, beating its naked breast angrily. At the same time, Brandon heard a sound in the undergrowth at his back. A swift glance over his shoulder made him draw a sharp breath. Breaking into view not a dozen yards away was Connie's lion.

The man and the lion saw each other at the same instant. With a nerve-shattering snarl in its throat, the tawny creature launched itself at Brandon. Brandon sidestepped in the nick of time. Then, as the lion spun round to attack him again, the gorilla squealed its defiance.

For a split second it was touch and go. Brandon saw the lion hesitate, torn between the man and the ape. It apparently decided that the ape was the greater prey, for it changed its direction and hurtled away to meet the clumsy form of the gorilla as it stepped off the bridge and lumbered forward to do battle.

For the thirty seconds that followed, Rex Brandon watched spellbound. Never had he seen such a ferocious contest, for the two great beasts were intent on destroying each other. Both were kings of the jungle, and for a full half-minute they fought tooth and fang to prove it.

Crouching motionless at the fringe of the undergrowth, Brandon watched as they struggled for mastery. The thick hairy arms of the ape almost tore the lion's jaws apart, but the raking claws of the powerful lion quickly put an end to that. Rolling over and over on the very brink of the ravine, the snarling animals were soon both bathed in their own blood. But in the end it was Connie's lion that won.

Leaping towards the ape in a terrific bound, its jaws snapped shut on the shaggy creature's throat. There was a fearful worrying noise as they tangled on the ground, then the lion jumped back, standing over its victim, breathing hard.

The gorilla made a weak effort to rise, then rolled over on its side, still and lifeless. The gentle slope of the ground took its dead carcase further and further towards the edge of the ravine till it suddenly vanished and dropped to the rocks out of sight.

Brandon got slowly to his feet, a wary eye on the triumphant lion. It was too busy licking its wounds to notice him yet, and he hoped to get across the bridge before it recovered. But before he had taken a step forward, the harsh nasal drawl of Raoul's voice rang in his ears: 'If you cross that bridge, you cross it dead! Stick your hands up!'

# 8

## Cobra Crag

The bitter taste of defeat was in Brandon's mouth as he turned his head slowly and faced up to Raoul. There was little humour in the man's expression, and the two automatics he held never shifted from their point of aim.

'Quite some little battle while it lasted, wasn't it?' he murmured grimly. 'I had you cold when it started, but I guess I got as interested as you did in what would happen.' He broke off and grinned. 'I was hoping the monk would win. I sure do hate that cat of Connie's!'

Brandon said nothing.

Raoul went on: 'We rounded up the rest of your bunch, so there's no sense in you running off. We have the woman again, and she's plenty enough insurance that you stick around. *And* we know what the old man's toy is for!'

'Do you?' Brandon's voice was flat and unemotional. Raoul jerked his head. 'Get moving!' he ordered. Brandon shrugged wearily. He suddenly felt that fate was being unkind. Nor did he think that Raoul was lying when he said the others were prisoners again. There was no sound of the men beating the jungle now. Their task was probably done. He turned and made his way back to the ruins. At a distance behind himself and Raoul came the lion, limping and stopping every now and then to lick its wounds.

The journey was a short one, but it was among the bitterest Brandon had ever made; and when they finally reached the arena where Litzgor had been tortured, he saw that Raoul had not lied. Lined up against the rugged stonework of the ruins were Mike Dorton, Charmaine and Litzgor. The only face he did not see among the captives was that of Scheki.

Connie dominated the scene. She it was who covered the prisoners with a pistol. A number of the natives stood round in a circle, watching her respectfully from a distance. At the sight of Brandon returning with Raoul, she gave a laugh and said something to Charmaine in a sneering tone of voice. Brandon permitted himself to be pushed into line with his friends. The hands of all of them were securely tied.

'Now then!' said Connie firmly. 'Now we can understand one another.'

'You can understand one thing!' snapped Litzgor defiantly. 'You'll get nothing out of me, no matter what you try!'

She regarded him in silence for a moment, then smiled obliquely at Raoul. 'We shall see,' she murmured softly. 'We already know that your little gadget is an appliance for locating gold. I admit we discovered that by accident, as it were, but the fact remains that we know what it is. All we need to know now is the correct method of operating it, and the cooperation of Charmaine, who has a good idea of where the gold reef lies. We shall then be content, you understand?'

'You'll be content to rot, as far as I'm concerned!' snapped Litzgor vindictively.

She nodded gently. 'Your attitude only

makes it more difficult for Charmaine,' she said slowly. 'I'm sorry for her, but there it is. The solution to her well-being is in your own hands, gentlemen.'

Brandon glanced at Litzgor meaningfully. He knew quite well that Connie was perfectly capable of fulfilling her threat. Such an eventually must at all costs be avoided.

Litzgor started to say something more, but caught Brandon's eye. The meaning of the glance was obvious. Litzgor hesitated for a moment, then shrugged as if throwing in his hand. 'Very well,' he said in a surly tone. 'We agree to your terms.'

She inclined her head. 'You're more sensible than I gave you credit for,' she murmured with a disarming smile. 'And now you will be returned to your original cell, where a meal will be brought you. If any further attempt to escape is made, no mercy will be shown. You will all be shot on recapture. And remember that there is no way off this place except across the bridge, which will now be under constant guard. That *is* all.'

They were herded down through the

cellar passage entrance and finally thrust back into the cell from which they had escaped. It was a dismal little party who stared at one another in the torch-lit gloom of their prison. 'What's the idea of giving in so easily?' said Litzgor in an irritable voice.

'That woman would have no compunction in doing what she hinted at,' answered Brandon grimly. 'Besides, if we give in now, we shall get another chance to escape later on. If we stuck our toes in really hard, it would only mean we should all end up dead, or being ill-treated so badly that we shouldn't be fit for anything.'

'Hmmm. Maybe you're right,' admitted the inventor.

'They never caught Scheki,' said Dorton quietly.

'If I know him, they never will!' answered Brandon with a grim smile. 'He's no fool when it comes to jungle movement.'

It was Charmaine who broke the ensuing silence. 'The only trouble is that I *can't* help them to find this wretched gold vein,' she said unhappily. 'I only know the approximate area in which it lies. Tom gave me a vague picture of the country in which he'd prospected, but I can't just lead them to it! He only mentioned one landmark when we talked about the actual location. Connie naturally thinks I know all about it, but I don't, honestly.'

Brandon frowned. 'Never mind,' he said gently. 'If you can kid them on that you know the approximate location, that will serve its purpose. It'll get us out of this place.'

They fell silent as the door was opened and two of the warriors appeared with food and drink. Only then did Brandon and his friends realise how hungry and thirsty they were after all their desperate exertions and suffering.

An hour later, Connie visited them. Raoul, armed with his ever-ready automatics, hovered in the background. The lion was apparently taking life easy after its fight with the giant gorilla. They stared at Connie balefully. She smiled back at them in a sardonic fashion.

'So you're behaving yourselves?' she said. 'I'm glad. It makes everything so much simpler, doesn't it? Now this is what we propose to do. It's too late to start off today, but if Charmaine will give us an idea as to where this fabulous gold lies, we can leave in the morning. Under her guidance we can travel to the vein, when friend Litzgor will do his stuff with his latest invention.'

'We all go, of course,' put in Brandon firmly.

She raised her eyebrows. 'Why should you?' she replied.

'I shan't do my part unless we all go together,' said Charmaine determinedly. 'That's final, Connie!'

Connie shrugged. 'As you like,' she said. 'It all comes to the same thing in the long run. Dorton can help the professor. As for Brandon . . . I really don't know what he's good for except a few strong-man acts!' She smiled.

Brandon said: 'I happen to be a qualified geologist, in case you didn't realise it. I'll willingly give you expert advice if it means saving my own life and those of my friends.'

Connie smirked. Raoul gave a chuckle. Charmaine nodded complacently. 'You might be useful after all,' she admitted. 'Now then, Charmaine, which way do we go from here when we leave in the morning? Make sure you tell us the right way, too!'

She hesitated, frowning. 'It's west of here,' she said quietly. 'How far, I can't say exactly; but when we get to the right vicinity we shall see a landmark I can't mistake.'

'What is it?'

But Charmaine shook her head firmly. 'Not till we get there!' she countered stubbornly. 'You'll have to rely on my judgment till then.'

Connie stared at her hard for a moment. 'You'd better not try to play any funny tricks, my dear,' she said in a sugary voice. 'You wouldn't like the consequences.'

'We'll take that for granted,' answered Charmaine woman icily.

Connie nodded coldly. 'Right!' she said after a moment's pause. 'Get as much rest as you can tonight; we leave at dawn, and I'm afraid the journey will not be as comfortable as it might be for any of you.

131

Being prisoners, you will be tied by the wrists to ensure your remaining together.'

Brandon stifled a yawn. 'Spare us the details,' he said.

They were left alone after that. Even under the grim circumstances of their capture, it was not long before they fell asleep one after the other.

Nor did they wake till two of the natives opened the door and brought them another meal. Brandon glanced at his watch and gave a start. 'Good Lord,' he said, 'it's morning!'

'Living under the ground like this, it's impossible to tell day from night,' complained Dorton sourly. 'How do you feel, Charmaine? Fit for the guide-book tour?'

She smiled and rubbed the sleep from her eyes. Litzgor remained silent and taciturn. Brandon made the best of it and tried to keep his companions in a cheerful frame of mind. With Jan Litzgor it was uphill work, though Charmaine and Mike seemed happy enough to take things as they came. Brandon noticed that Charmaine was spending a lot of time in conversation with the good-looking Mike.

It gave him a pleasant feeling for some reason or other. They made a well-matched pair, he reflected.

'How far do you reckon we are from this virgin gold field?' he asked her presently.

She shrugged. 'Honestly, Rex, I haven't an idea,' she admitted. 'Not above fifty miles, I should say.'

'Pleasant thought,' murmured Dorton wearily. 'Fifty long miles! What a trip!'

'It's probably a lot less than that,' she said consolingly. 'I just don't know.'

They were taken from the cellar a few minutes later. Once in the open air, their hands were tied at the wrists and they were each attached to a long rope. Brandon reflected sourly that it was rather like being a member of a chain gang. Raoul, Connie, half a dozen of the native warriors and the lion completed the party, the natives acting as bearers.

Brandon was destined to remember the journey they made with many bitter recollections. It was one of the grimmest and most uncomfortable he had ever undertaken. For a whole week they trekked through jungle, swamp and broken mountain country. The breaks were short, and the only thing in Connie's favour was the fact that she insisted that her prisoners should be well fed. Even that was cancelled out by the discomfort of being roped together for several hours at a stretch while on the move.

At noon on the seventh day, Charmaine suddenly stopped in her tracks. Brandon, following her, nearly collided with her.

'What's the matter?' asked Dorton anxiously.

'Cobra crag,' she whispered, starting forward again. 'See it? Way ahead there, a little to the left of that rising mist. That's my landmark — a great crag of rock in the shape of a cobra's head with its hood extended!' She could not hide the natural excitement that crept into her voice.

'Quiet,' urged Brandon. 'Don't let them know yet. We want to think this out carefully.' She nodded, saying nothing more.

Brandon watched the writhing tendrils of mist that rose in the distance. He was puzzled by them, and not a little troubled by the sulphurous heat which had recently clamped down on the scrubland through which they were plodding. From the expressions on the faces of the natives, he realised that they, too, were uneasy. Keeping his thoughts to himself, he decided that the safari was entering a volcanic belt of dangerous mountain country.

That evening they had almost reached the giant sculptured rock that thrust up through a sea of undergrowth in the form of a great cobra's head. When Raoul and Connie called a halt for the night, it was on the edge of what appeared to be another stretch of swamp. Camp was made, but it was not until everyone had settled down after the evening meal that they had misgivings about the spot they had chosen as a resting place. From beyond the swamp came a grumbling sound that was followed a moment later by the distinct noise of bubbling water.

Raoul scowled and glanced at Connie. 'Don't like the sound of that,' he said. 'I'll take a couple of the men and have a look-see.'

'Watch your step,' advised Connie quietly.

Brandon said nothing. The mystery of

the bubbling sound was not quite as deep to him; he had heard the same sort of thing before in his wanderings.

Raoul set off, disappearing into the thick shadows that clung around the base of the giant crag of rock. When he returned, his face was uneasy in the firelight. Speaking in low tones to Connie, he said: 'This is some spot. There's a lake of boiling mud at the bottom of that darned great rock over yonder! We worked our way round the swamp here and came on it suddenly. Near enough fell in, too! I guess this is volcanic territory.'

Her mouth hardened visibly as she stared back at him. 'If that woman's tricked me, she'll be sorry!' she said in a venomous undertone. 'Charmaine, is this the right way?'

Brandon nudged her. 'Better tell her about the crag,' he whispered. 'Don't give anything more away if you can help it.'

She stared up at Connie as the woman approached. 'That crag is my landmark,' she said quietly. 'I've never been here before, remember. I'm only going on what Tom told me. That's Cobra Crag;

we're on the right track.'

Connie nodded curtly, turning away and rejoining Raoul outside the small tent they had brought along with them.

The night passed uneventfully, but with the resumption of the trek at dawn they quickly ran into even tougher going than previously. Skirting the bubbling mass of boiling mud which formed a grim lake at the base of the cobra-headed crag, the party kept edging further and further to the north. Charmaine, when questioned closely by Connie, admitted that to the best of her knowledge the gold reef was reputed to lie several miles to the north of the crag.

'I've also been told that it's some of the most dangerous country in the world,' she added cheerfully.

'You'll be sharing the dangers with us,' retorted the other woman swiftly.

Brandon eyed the mass of boiling mud. It was from here that the wreaths of steam had been rising in the form of mist when they first set eyes on the place. He did not like the look of it at all, for with boiling mud actually on the surface it spoke of unstable volcanic conditions in the neighbourhood. However, there was no sense in raising the fears of his friends, so he held his tongue.

After an hour's trek through thin undergrowth and over hard, rocky ground that was semi-desert in nature, they were brought up short by evidence of previous volcanic disturbance. Great fissures had opened in the ground, completely barring their routes and forcing them to sidetrack for considerable distances. It was while they were making one of these detours in order to cross the end of a particularly lengthy fissure that Brandon spotted prints in the sandy ground which gave him grave misgivings and caused him to glance round warily. Brandon was not the only man in the party to see the signs.

One of the men spoke urgently to Raoul, who frowned. Connie demanded to know what the trouble was. Blind to danger, she was forcing the pace in her eagerness to reach the fabulous goal she had set herself.

'What's going on?' breathed Charmaine in a whisper.

Brandon decided to be frank about it. 'They've just seen footprints in the sand,' he answered. 'If you ask me, this outfit is up against more than it bargained for. Unless they watch out, they'll be jumped by hostile natives. In this place they're not likely to be friendly ones!'

Charmaine shuddered.

Passing through broken ground amid rocks, boulders, tropic scrub and stunted undergrowth, the safari wound onwards. At every turn it seemed that fresh fissures in the ground set them back on another tack. Even Brandon lost his sense of direction, until a glance at the now distant Cobra Crag put him right.

And then, without any warning, they came on the men. Before Raoul or Connie had time to realise it, a group of armed and painted warriors were rushing to meet them, shouting and screaming as they came.

# 9

## Tribe of the Gold God

It was fortunate for the small safari party that they did not happen to be in an exposed position at the time of the attack. Had they been, nothing could have saved them from being wiped out. As it was, there was just sufficient time to get their backs against a shallow cliff and avoid being surrounded.

Raoul and Connie, together with their half dozen men, quickly stemmed the first tide of assault. The crash of their automatics was almost continuous, interspersed by the sharper crackle of the rifles carried by the bearers. But their attackers were numerous and the odds against the party great.

Brandon and his fellow prisoners were in a fever of dread at being caught in this situation. Being tied, they were helpless to defend themselves; and with spears and clubs whistling through the air and clanging against the rock at their backs, every second was fraught with danger.

'Why don't you let us free?' shouted Dorton to Raoul.

'You shut up!' snapped the man. He did not even bother to look round, but went on firing with both his automatics at the natives as they hurled themselves forward. Brandon gritted his teeth as a spear crashed into the ground close beside him. He glanced at it, blinking at what he saw. The blade of the weapon was fashioned from pure gold. He saw, too, that their shields were also of gold, crudely beaten.

The situation was rapidly deteriorating. Three of the men had been wounded and one was dead. Even Raoul and Connie were getting worried.

'Cut us loose and we'll help!' said Brandon grimly. Connie threw him a startled glance. She seemed uncertain as to what to do. Then another attack, fiercer than any of the previous ones, turned the balance. Leaving the defence to Raoul for an instant, she raced to where the prisoners crouched against the rock at their backs.

'On parole!' she snapped. 'Use the men's rifles!' As she spoke, she whipped out a hunting knife and slashed at their bonds.

'Thanks!' Brandon and the rest did not wait for more. Grabbing up the rifles of the fallen men, they began firing at the oncoming natives. It was a wonderful relief to have a gun in his hands again.

The fresh and more deadly fire had an immediate effect on their attackers. But it was not only the rifle fire which turned the scales. Connie's lion, which had not been idle during the preceding minutes, was wreaking havoc in the ranks of the natives. Snarling and roaring, it brought down and slaughtered man after man, oblivious to the spears that were hurled at it. Urged on by Connie's shouts, the great tawny beast proved a valuable ally to the hard-pressed party.

Brandon picked out one of the warriors who appeared to be the leader of the repeated attacks. 'Concentrate on that one!' he snapped to the others. 'If we get him, they'll break, I think!'

A veritable hail of bullets sung out from their rifles. Raoul and Connie, too, heard what Brandon said. They fired as fast as they could at the gesticulating figure of the leader.

Riddled by bullets, the native dropped to the ground, clawing the dirt in his dying agony. Even as he breathed his last, he was shouting to his comrades in a tongue that Brandon could not understand.

But the loss of their leader was the turning point of the battle as far as the men were concerned. Harried by more accurate shooting on the part of Brandon and the remainder of the party, and tormented by the terror of the native lion, they started to retreat, finally turning and fleeing in a panic as several more of their number fell.

'We did it!' gasped Raoul triumphantly. He looked at Brandon and the other prisoners, now armed and loose. A look of uneasiness crossed his face. For long seconds the two parties stared at each other. Unconsciously their guns were trained on their enemies. It was a deadlock of sorts, for neither could claim the advantage. Raoul, Connie and the two remaining men covered Brandon, Dorton, Charmaine and Jan Litzgor.

'Stalemate!' murmured Brandon. 'You needn't think we'll give up our guns now!'

Connie glared at him venomously. 'You were released on parole,' she snapped.

'But we never gave our parole,' said Dorton firmly. 'It was your idea.'

Brandon grinned. 'Whether we like it or not,' he said, 'we're allies in this thing for the time being. Don't imagine that we've seen the last of those natives. They'll be back in even greater numbers, and if you've any sense you'll get a move on and find a safer place than this.'

Raoul's jaw tightened. 'I've a good mind to shoot you, Brandon!' he snarled.

'The fewer there are of us, the smaller chance we shall have of surviving,' pointed out Brandon reasonably. 'We're up against a common enemy now, my friend.'

Connie gave a curt nod. 'He's right,' she said. 'Very well, we'll play it your way, strongman — for the moment at any rate.'

'I suggest we move,' he said flatly.

They continued on their way, watchful for any signs of a fresh attack by the natives. At last they managed to extricate themselves from the fissure-broken ground, reaching an area of narrow, scrub-grown wadis and shallow ravines. Here and there dense clumps of foliage sprouted from the hot, moist soil. At one point Brandon caught sight of another pool of steaming liquid mud. There was a sulphurous tang in the atmosphere.

Making their way along the floor of a winding ravine, they headed north. They continued for a long time, till suddenly the ravine ended abruptly as it turned a sharp right angle. Brandon came to a halt, staring about worriedly. He did not like the look of the situation, for at this point the sides of the ravine were almost sheer and quite unclimbable. Turning to Connie, he frowned. She seemed to have more initiative than Raoul, and was naturally co-leader of the party with Brandon.

'We'll have to go back as quickly as we can,' said Brandon. 'We're in a death trap here.'

She gave him an admiring glance which brought a scowl of jealousy to Raoul's face. Then: 'Yes,' she agreed.

They turned and started back in the opposite direction. Brandon recalled having seen a place at which the sides of the ravine could be scaled some half-mile back. But long before they reached it, the thing which Brandon had dreaded happened.

With a wild shrill chorus of cries, a small army of natives charged into view. They were led by one of the tallest men any of the whites had ever seen, and they came on with relentless determination and fanatical disregard for their lives.

Caught in the deadly trap of the narrow box-ended ravine, the party started shooting with desperate accuracy. Their new attackers were far more numerous than previously, and even Brandon, optimist though he was, realised that they stood little chance of getting away a second time.

Aided by Connie's lion, the party put up a reckless fight. But the remaining two men were killed in the first phase of the battle. The loss of their firepower turned the scales in favour of the enemy. Litzgor was stunned by a club, and Raoul went down with an injured arm, his twin automatics silent.

Fighting to the last ounce of their combined strength, the little party was overrun. Something struck Brandon on the back of the head, and he knew nothing more. His last vision of the scene was one of confusion, and a vivid impression of Charmaine being grasped in the arms of a native as she struggled to escape. Then, with a violent shouting in his ears, everything went black.

When he opened his eyes again, it was to find himself lying on the ground, hands and feet securely tied. All round him was darkness, but far overhead he could make out the stars of a hot night sky. Somewhere close there was a groaning noise.

Brandon struggled over onto his side and peered round painfully. His head was aching abominably, but he fought down the waves of sickness that swept across his brain. He had to find out what the position was.

By straining his eyes in the thick gloom,

he made out the recumbent forms of several other people nearby. One of them was groaning dismally. After a few minutes' concentration on his surroundings, he was able to piece together a clear enough picture of what had happened.

The entire party were lying there bound hand and foot. It seemed to Brandon that they had been dumped in a wooden stockade or compound, and the place was almost certainly in the heart of a native kraal. Beyond the thick wooden walls of the place, he could hear the voices of natives and the monotonous beat of a drum. The glow of fires shimmered on the foliage of trees where they showed above the stockade top.

Rolling towards the nearest form on the ground, he discovered it was Dorton. Beyond Dorton lay Raoul, groaning softly. A check on the rest proved that the party were there, but the lion had either been killed or had escaped.

It was Connie who threw fresh light on their position. Speaking bitterly, she told Brandon that for several minutes she had listened to their captors discussing their fate. Apparently the local dialect was not entirely strange to her, being akin in many respects to the tongue of her own men. 'We're in for trouble in a big way,' she said. 'This is the native village, and they worship an idol made of solid gold. I wasn't unconscious when they brought us in, so I saw it. Later on tonight, there's going to be a feast, and we shall then be sacrificed.'

'Hmm . . . It looks bad, doesn't it,' said Brandon. He worked his way across to Charmaine. She had not been hurt, and was far more cheerful than he expected her to be.

Time passed slowly, with every minute made worse by the fact that they could hear the preparations going on outside the compound. An enormous fire had been lit, and already the dirge-like sounds of singing rose hideous in the night. Just when it seemed that there was nothing to do but wait for their fate to come, Brandon's sharp ears caught a sound which brought his heart to his mouth. From the darker side of the stockade came the whisper of a man's voice and a slight grating noise.

Brandon rolled across the ground as quickly as he could. With his head against the wall of pointed stakes, he dared to speak. The noise of cautious movement was repeated, closer this time. Then a well-remembered voice answered Brandon's whispered query.

'It is I, Scheki. You must escape before it is too late.'

'Thank the Lord you managed to trail us,' answered Brandon. 'But we can't escape without help.'

'I pass a knife between the stakes, *bwana*,' came Scheki's muttered reply. 'Turn on your side so that the blade will cut your bonds.'

Brandon did as he was told. The gaps between the wooden stakes of the compound were wide enough to permit Scheki's knife to enter. By careful manipulation, Brandon succeeded in rubbing his wrists against the keen edge of the knife. After a torturing few minutes, the ropes parted company and his hands were free.

'Thanks, Scheki,' he breathed. 'Now give me the knife and I'll free the rest.'

'It is good, *bwana*.'

Brandon, free to move about now, silently released the remainder of the captives. He paused when he came to Raoul. 'I've a good mind to leave you tied up,' he said grimly.

The man's drawn face was suddenly scared. 'You couldn't do a thing like that!' he gasped.

'No, I guess I couldn't.' He cut Raoul loose.

'What's your plan?' whispered Litzgor grimly. He was holding something in his hand, something that Brandon had not seen before. Then he remembered that after freeing Litzgor, his back had been turned. Litzgor had been close to Connie. Now he was holding the small apparatus which had been the primary cause of all the trouble. Connie herself did not seem to care anymore.

Brandon thought for a moment. Then: 'We must wait till they come for us,' he said. 'Then we attack and fight our way out — if we can.'

Litzgor and the others nodded. Dorton was close to the inventor, who was opening his precious electronic device with a view to testing it. Raoul and Connie looked on with fresh interest.

Brandon made his way across the compound to the wall where he had left Scheki. The knowledge that his faithful colleague was still alive and well was the best piece of news he had had in years. He knew instinctively that they owed their lives to Scheki's loyalty. But first of all they must escape from the stockade and reach the friendly cover of the jungle growth nearby.

Calling in a whisper, he contacted Scheki again, hearing the story of how he had followed them as closely as possible ever since the moment of their recapture by Raoul. Scheki had another plan for escape, which he also mentioned to Brandon.

'It might be better, *bwana*, if you and the rest scaled the wall at the back here. Is there anyone too badly injured to do that?'

Brandon, whose main intention had been to lay hands on some of the natives' weapons, thought for a moment, deciding in the end that Scheki's idea was a good one. 'We can all get over the stockade,' he said slowly. 'It's high, but we can help one another.'

'You must hurry, *inkosi*,' said Scheki quietly. 'There is much activity round the campfire and in front of the golden idol.'

Brandon returned quickly to the others, to find them gathered in a silent but excited group round Litzgor.

'What's going on?' he whispered urgently. 'We've no time to waste; we're getting out of here!'

Charmaine turned a pale face towards him. 'Jan says there's a very rich gold deposit directly underneath this place!' she answered. 'His little machine recorded it!'

Brandon muttered noncommittally. 'Interesting,' he said. 'But not of great importance at the moment, I'm afraid. Come with me, all of you!'

They followed him like sheep, dominated by his sense of leadership and the urgency of his tone. Under his direction, Mike Dorton and Litzgor climbed the palisade and were given a hand down by Scheki. Once he had a couple of his own people across, Brandon ordered Raoul and Connie to follow. Then it was Charmaine's turn.

Listening, Brandon heard the sound of many approaching footsteps coming towards the entrance gate of the compound. 'Up you go,' he whispered. He lifted Charmaine and gave her time to grip the top of the palisade, then heaved her further up by the ankles. She straddled the top uncomfortably and stayed there, peering down at him.

There was a sudden rattling noise at the gate and the sound of many voices being raised in a sort of ceremonial chant. Brandon clenched his teeth and leapt for the top. His fingers closed on the rough wood. Charmaine reached down a hand and grasped his wrist.

'Get down the other side!' he breathed urgently. 'I'm all right.' But she hung on, determined to help him.

Brandon squirmed up and swung his legs across the top. As he did so, the gateway of the stockade creaked open, and it was at that critical moment that Charmaine gave a gasp of dismay and grabbed wildly at Brandon. He tried to save her from falling, but to his horror she slipped from his grasp, the sleeve of her bush shirt tearing loose in his fingers. With a muttered curse, Brandon himself overbalanced in an effort to stop her falling. Next moment he had landed heavily among his fellow fugitives, while Charmaine's cry rose loudly from inside the stockade as the natives caught sight of her.

Ready hands seized Brandon and dragged him to his feet. He found Mike Dorton at his side.

'Come on!' urged Dorton desperately. 'They're coming to look for us.'

Brandon shook his head to clear it. 'They've got Charmaine,' he gasped. 'She stayed to give me a hand and fell.'

'Let's get clear,' said Litzgor. 'We can come back for her. If we stay here, we shan't stand a chance.'

Brandon hated the idea, but there was nothing else for it. Under the guidance of Scheki, they sprinted for the dark cover of the jungle fringe twenty or thirty yards distant. By now the entire kraal was in uproar, natives running this way and that, shouting to one another as they sought for the prisoners. But in spite of their easy break-out, Brandon was sick at heart as he remembered Charmaine's despairing cry when she fell almost into the arms of the enemy.

Not until they reached the security of the jungle growth did they pause for breath. Then they stared back at the scene in the village. Seen from a distance like this, it was not reassuring. The first thing Brandon sighted was the figure of Charmaine being marched out of the stockade in the middle of a group of a dozen warriors. They were making straight for the fantastic idol that was set up on the far side of a circular space in the centre of the kraal. In front of the idol was a great fire, the dancing flames of which reflected dully on the yellow metal of the image.

'We've got to do something to save her,' said Dorton in a desperate whisper. 'Rex, give me that knife; I'm going in there.'

'You're doing nothing of the sort,' answered Brandon firmly. 'You're in charge till I join the party again. Get everyone clear of this place and start back for Cobra Crag.'

Dorton tried to argue, but Brandon was adamant. He said there was no time to lose. Already Charmaine was being led towards the hideous golden idol, in front of which a weirdly garbed figure was waiting to receive her.

'The local witch doctor,' breathed Litzgor.

'Scheki,' said Brandon urgently, 'get them away. I'll see you later.'

'*Yebbo, inkosi,*' said the black very quietly. Brandon waited for no more, but started to skirt round the edge of the village while the rest of the party faded out in the darkness.

Barely had they left the scene before Brandon felt the earth quiver beneath his feet. Then there was a loud rumbling noise and a violent hissing sound. With a feeling of instinctive fear, he realised he was up against volcanic elements as well as idol-worshipping natives. But the life of Charmaine was in deadly peril. Nothing must prevent him from reaching her.

Grasping his knife, he hurried on.

Again a heavy tremor ran through the earth on which he trod. The air was thick with a sulphurous reek, and there were signs of dismay among the gathering of natives in the centre of the kraal.

# 10

## The Earthquake

By the time Brandon arrived at the rear of the golden idol and peered cautiously out from the cover of a derelict hut, the scene had altered considerably. Filled with terror by the quaking of the ground, the natives were dancing feverishly round in front of the witch doctor. Two of them were grasping Charmaine by the arms, and by the sound of the general clamour that was going on, Brandon guessed that they were urging the witch doctor to sacrifice her before it was too late. Plainly the gold god was angry with them over something; the earth was heaving.

Wondering desperately how he could rescue the hapless woman, Brandon crept round the side of the hut. It was then that he had his first stroke of real luck. Leaning against the wall of the little building was an old spear, its shaft broken about halfway down. It was a poor weapon, but better than the knife he had.

The witch doctor seemed to be almost as frightened as the rest of the natives. Then it seemed to Brandon that he made up his mind. Taking a great flat sword from a stand in front of the golden idol, he advanced on the cowering figure of Charmaine.

Brandon knew that he must act immediately. He left the cover of the tumbledown hut and strode forward, the broken spear raised in his hand.

Almost at once there was a shout of anger as the natives caught sight of the intruder. Brandon did not wait. He stopped abruptly, poised the spear above his head, and sent it hurtling through the air straight at the witch doctor.

There was a high-pitched scream as the golden blade buried itself in the man's naked neck. Just as he had been about to plunge his sacrificial sword into Charmaine, he was struck down.

Immediately pandemonium broke loose. The warriors, incensed by what Brandon had done, started forward in a body. Brandon saw that Charmaine was still held by her two guards, but that the natives were glancing this way and that in fear and wonderment. And that was all he had time to notice, for the yelling men were intent on killing him for what he had done. Turning and running to save his own life, he pelted for cover. But no sooner had he plunged into the undergrowth of the jungle before there was a sudden screaming from the kraal. It was followed an instant later by the deep-throated roar of a lion and a fearful worrying noise.

Brandon stopped in his tracks, hardly daring to believe his ears. Surely, he thought, Connie's lion hadn't turned up to give him a hand?

The men who had started after him also stopped, peering back at the village. What they saw made them pause. Then with one accord, they turned on their heels and raced back into the village, the lone man forgotten in this new peril that threatened their women and children.

Brandon gave them a few seconds' start, then he too made for the kraal again. Arriving on the edge of the jungle, he saw that it was indeed Connie's great cat that was wreaking havoc among the inhabitants. Its flashing fangs and claws had already done several of the natives to death, and it was at the moment in the act of springing on the back of a screaming woman as she tried to run from it.

Brandon searched for Charmaine. He saw her struggling to escape from the grip of one of the warriors as the man tried to drag her towards the great fire in front of the golden idol. Turning a blind eye to all danger, Brandon raced forward, his hunting knife flashing in the firelight as he raised it ready to strike.

But yet another ally was to come to his aid. With a sudden explosive roar, the whole earth seemed to lift and drop again. Huts collapsed at the edge of the kraal; the cries of women and children mingled with the startled yells of the warriors. Then a ten-foot-high fountain of boiling mud erupted from the very centre of the village and spouted upwards in a torrent of scalding death.

The man who was dragging Charmaine away gave a yelp of terror and let her go, fleeing from this peril that he did not understand. The volcanic eruption threw the natives into complete and utter confusion. It also scared off the lion and sent it skittering out of range with a low growl of fear.

Brandon reached Charmaine's side just as the spouting mud shot upwards again, this time on a much bigger scale. A river of boiling stuff, gleaming red hot in the gloom of night, began to spread across the ground.

Grabbing Charmaine by the wrist, Brandon drew her away. 'Run like the devil!' he shouted above the din.

With the river of boiling mud drawing perilously close to their heels, the two of them fled from the kraal, heading for the jungle with the cries and screams of burned and tortured natives ringing in their ears. Not until they were well away from the vicinity of the village did Brandon pause for breath. Charmaine more or less collapsed on the quivering earth, sobbing gratefully.

Brandon frowned, peering round in the darkness. His watch told him that day should be breaking shortly, but the sky was so overcast and thick that the darkness persisted. And still the quivering went on beneath his feet. He thought the whole area must be active and that other eruptions would be sure to break through at frequent intervals. It was no place to linger in, and urging Charmaine to her feet again he led the way back in the direction of Cobra Crag, the deep and ominous sound of the earthquake still echoing from the stricken village.

'Sorry we had to leave you in the lurch,' said Brandon as they started off again. 'I sent the rest on to Cobra Crag. We should catch them up before long.'

Charmaine had by now pulled herself together. She carried a spear she had wrenched from a dead native. Brandon still had his knife. They plunged on through the dense jungle, making the best time they could.

After about a mile of difficult progress, a stealthy sound in the undergrowth and scrub ahead made Brandon halt. From the darkness, a tall dark form materialised, stopping when it caught sight of the two people.

'All is well, *bwana*,' said Scheki quietly. 'I leave the *bwana* Dorton in charge of the two bad *mulungus* and come to find you and the lady. Let us go.'

'Good to see you again,' murmured Brandon with a sigh of relief. 'I don't think we shall see any more of the natives. The whole place was being destroyed by an earthquake when we last set eyes on them!'

'There is much angry earth movement, *inkosi*,' said Scheki with a nervous shudder. 'I am afraid of it.'

'Where did you leave the others?' asked Charmaine, changing the subject quickly.

'Missy, they are on the edge of one of those swamps of boiling and bubbling mud. Not very far away now, I think.'

'It's a pity Raoul and Connie didn't walk straight into it in that case,' she said. 'They've brought us more trouble than anything else. Rex, I can't tell you how sorry I am for all this business. If it hadn't been for me, you'd never have had to risk your life the way you have.'

'My dear lady,' he said quietly, 'you might as well forget it. Litzgor was determined to get back his gadget, and that alone entailed our mixing it with your sister-in-law and her boyfriend! This is as much our game as it is yours. The only difference is that you had a greater stake in the affair than we did.'

'You're a very generous man, aren't you?' she said in a surprisingly tender voice.

Brandon could find no suitable answer to that so kept quiet.

When they finally arrived at the hot swamp of mud, the light of day was beginning to break through the clouds of smoke and volcanic haze that hung above the earth. Scheki raised an arm and pointed to a place some distance from where they had emerged at the edge of the jungle. 'Over there, *bwana*. That is where I leave the others.'

Brandon nodded curtly. He stared through the grey light of dawn, making out a small group of figures some twenty yards away. Just as he sighted them, he halted dead in his tracks, laying a silencing hand on Charmaine's arm. 'Something wrong there,' he muttered grimly.

Scheki stared hard at the group of

people. Brandon quickly made out Dorton and Litzgor. The other two were Connie and Raoul. But it was plain at a glance that instead of Dorton and his friend being masters of the situation, the tables had been turned. Raoul gripped a long-shafted spear in both hands. He held it pointing straight at Litzgor's stomach, the tip of the blade only inches from the man. And Dorton and Litzgor were backing slowly but surely towards the sea of bubbling, steaming mud at their backs.

Charmaine drew a sharp breath of dismay as she saw and understood what was going on. But worse was to come. Without any warning, the tawny shape of Connie's lion came loping into view. It must have taken a different route from the devastated village to that followed by Brandon and Charmaine. Now it had come to rejoin its mistress.

'She'll set it on them!' gasped Charmaine desperately. 'Rex, we've got to stop it!' Her fingers were clutching at his arm in sudden fear. Scheki looked at his employer.

Brandon said: 'Stay right here, Charmaine. We'll deal with this. Don't move an inch, remember; I don't want to lose you again.' She nodded wordlessly.

Brandon and Scheki moved off, keeping out of sight as they advanced on the group of four people at the edge of the volcanic swamp. Things were getting desperate with Dorton and Litzgor, for Raoul was gradually forcing them closer and closer to the bubbling mud. Gouts of steam puffed up from it at intervals, and a heavy mist of stinking fumes hung above it. If a man put his foot in that, thought Brandon, it would be the end.

They were ten or a dozen yards in the rear of Raoul and Connie when she spoke to the lion and stroked its tawny mane. Instantly the great beast started to move towards the two trapped men. Litzgor shouted something out. There was stark fear in his voice, but Connie only laughed.

'Now!' whispered Brandon.

He and Scheki darted out from the cover of the scrub and raced towards Raoul and Connie. But the lion, which had almost reached Dorton and was crouched to spring, heard or scented them before they could reach their goal. It turned, snarling, on its haunches, then launched itself straight as an arrow for Brandon.

'Get 'em if you can, Scheki!' said Brandon. He halted where he was, waiting for the impact of the lion's attack. All he had to defend himself with was the hunting knife Scheki had given him in the compound. Now his very life depended on it, for he could not look for much assistance from Scheki, who had his hands full the moment the two had caught sight of him.

Then the lion was on him. He stepped to one side and lunged with the knife, sinking the blade in its flesh as it whirled past and stopped. Darting round, he prepared for a second charge, knowing that unless he found a vital spot in the creature's body, the end would come quickly. Already tired and close to exhaustion, his strength was flagging.

The lion crouched, snarling, its wicked yellow eyes fixed unblinkingly on Brandon. Then it leapt, the full weight of its powerful body landing squarely on Brandon's chest. They went down together, razor-sharp claws raking the flesh from Brandon's upper arms as he struggled to free himself sufficiently to use the knife. When he did manage to get one arm free, the lion's reeking jaws were close to his throat. In an instant it would be tearing at his flesh. He brought up the knife and rammed it deep in the creature's neck.

The lion gave a convulsive heave and roared in a mixture of pain and fury. Brandon took the only chance there was and dragged himself from underneath the weight of its quivering body.

But Connie's great cat was by no means finished. Wounded though it was, it leapt up and threw itself into the fight again, intent on killing the man who had dared to pit his puny strength against its mighty sinews.

Brandon, gasping for breath and with the sweat pouring from every inch of his skin, turned to face the oncoming brute. The impact of the lion when it struck him almost carried him to the ground again, but by a tremendous exertion of his muscles he succeeded in keeping his feet.

At the same instant he drove home the long blade of the knife in the lion's side.

There was a split second when he felt the hot breath of the killer on his face, but by twisting round a little he got a grip on its hairy throat with his left hand, while again and again he stabbed and twisted with the knife. The warm blood of his own wounds mingled with that of the lion, running down his arm and spattering the ground over which they fought.

Dimly he heard the voice of Connie shouting encouragement to the lion. Dorton, too, was yelling. But he had no time to see what the situation was in that direction. All he knew was that he had to kill the great cat before it killed him, and a moment later he realised the battle for life was over. The lion's head suddenly sagged over sideways, the full weight of its body going limp against him as the knife found the animal's heart and stilled it forever.

Brandon exerted all his strength and forced the body back so that it toppled slowly over and crashed to the ground with a dead-sounding thud. Then his own knees gave way, and he sank in an exhausted and semiconscious heap at the side of the slaughtered king of the jungle.

# 11

## 'They're Out For Blood!'

How long the blackout lasted Brandon never knew, but it could only have been a matter of seconds; then he was fully conscious again and aware of a confusion of sound not far from where he lay. Leaning up on one elbow, he glanced round. The dead carcase of the lion was so close that he could reach out and touch its magnificent mane. But there were other matters to occupy his attention. The picture as he saw it was very different to what he had expected.

Dorton and Litzgor were still standing with their backs to the steaming swamp of mud. Its bubbling surface formed a grim background to the drama being enacted between Brandon and them.

Scheki, with a brief glance over his shoulder, saw that Brandon had recovered. Raoul and Connie were close together. She held the small case of Litzgor's invention in her hand and raised it high. 'If you don't get out of the way, I'll toss it in the mud!' she spat at Scheki.

Raoul still threatened Litzgor with his spear. And poor Scheki did not quite know what to do. Nor could either Dorton or Litzgor go to his aid, for the threat of Raoul's weapon held them stationary on the edge of the swamp. Connie's eyes were fierce as she glared at Scheki. Then Brandon staggered to his feet and weaved dizzily in towards the stalemated group.

'It's all up, Connie!' he snapped. 'Why don't you throw in your hand and be sensible? I've killed your lion, so it can't come and help you now.'

'I'll kill you for that — among other things!' she said.

'I doubt it,' he answered dryly. He still held the knife with which he had finished the lion. Taking it by the tip of its blade, he balanced it carefully between his fingers. 'I can throw these things pretty accurately,' he said.

'If you do, I'll throw this!' she retorted vindictively.

'That wouldn't save Raoul.'

'What do I care for Raoul? And where's that precious little woman you've been dragging around? Have you lost her to the natives at last?'

Brandon shook his head slowly. He did not want to risk the loss of Litzgor's invention if he could help it, though the thing meant little enough to him personally.

'She's around,' he told Connie. His eyes were darting from side to side. If Dorton moved like lightning, he thought, he and Litzgor might get away with it. Raoul was in no state to act really fast. He tried to work it out, but his own brain was beginning to swim again. He must have lost a lot of blood, he reflected uneasily. Could he move quickly enough for what he had to do? he wondered. The lake of bubbling mud gave a convulsive shudder behind Mike Dorton and Litzgor. Instinctively they turned their heads in a frightened fashion.

Brandon took the chance offered. With a lightning move, he leapt at Connie, grabbing her arm and forcing it down so that she let out a squeal of pain. At the same time Scheki threw himself forward and wound one arm round Raoul's neck from the rear, dragging him over backwards. Then Dorton and the inventor sprang away from the edge of the mud swamp as it gave another heave. It looked as if the tables were turned once again. But as Brandon went down on top of Connie, the earth beneath them shook and quaked so that he was almost thrown over sideways. Connie was fighting like a cat, biting and scratching. Brandon had a fleeting impulse to laugh, for it struck him that this was even worse than handling a lion. And he could not very well make use of his knife on a woman, either. Even one like Connie.

The little invention dropped from her fingers and rolled away. Litzgor sprang forward and picked it up triumphantly. Then there was a sudden eruption of noise and steam from the mud. Before Brandon fully realised what was happening, he felt himself spattered with scalding gouts of liquid fire. In the pain of his burns he let go of Connie and jumped to his feet. The woman gave a cry as some of the spouting mud landed on her chest. In an instant she was up. The earth shook and rocked where they stood. So violent was the quake that Litzgor and Dorton both fell to the ground. Brandon staggered sideways dizzily. He caught a glimpse of Scheki's startled face as he leapt back from Raoul. Then Connie darted in towards Litzgor, wrenched his invention from his fingers and started running for her life away from the edge of the swamp.

Raoul, after a moment's hesitation during which he did not realise he was no longer a prisoner of Scheki, lumbered after her.

Dorton and Litzgor were slow to rise, for the ground was still writhing in a series of great, deep-seated shudders. As for Brandon, he could barely stand, and was so dizzy that he thought he would fall at any moment.

Only Scheki seemed unaffected to any extent. He it was who grasped Brandon's arm and dragged him clear of the edge of the mud swamp just in time. Dorton and

Litzgor followed at an unsteady run. Behind them the whole surface of heaving mud burst upwards, showering the foliage nearby with a hail of burning liquid earth. Only the trees saved them all from frightful burns. By the time they stopped running, there was no sign of Raoul or Connie.

'We've got to get them!' said Litzgor insistently. 'My invention!'

'Damn your invention!' snapped Brandon. 'Charmaine's about somewhere. I hope she's all right.'

Scheki darted off in a different direction, calling as he went. The rest of them waited, feeling and hearing the increasing tremors of the disrupted earth.

Scheki appeared with Ccarmaine. She was unhurt, having taken refuge in the jungle when the mud erupted.

'Now we'll go after the others!' said Brandon grimly.

'Which way?'

'They're bound to make for Cobra Crag. We've all got to go in that direction if we want to get out of this mess.' Even as he spoke, there was another violent upheaval from the swamp. The air was thick with steam and choking fumes. Over their heads they could hear the spatter of falling debris on the leaves. Terrified animals raced through the jungle, fleeing from a fate beyond their comprehension.

Moving as quickly as they could under the difficult conditions, the party set off. Scheki and Brandon were in the lead, with Dorton, Litzgor and Charmaine bringing up the rear.

Little was said by any one, for they were all at the limits of fatigue, pale and drawn about the face and unsteady on their feet as they forced a way through the undergrowth or crossed the numerous patches of burning-hot sand and skirted fissures in the ground.

It was when they were threading a way in and out among the volcanic fissures where they had so nearly perished once before that fate again put them to the test. Skirting the edge of a particularly deep ravine, Brandon came to a sudden halt, listening anxiously. From not far away came a drumming sound which grew in intensity as the seconds passed.

'*Bwana*,' murmured Scheki, 'there is danger.' The others crowded round, peering this way and that as they tried to locate the source of the ominous noise.

Charmaine gave a sudden cry of alarm, pointing away to the right. Brandon saw a small herd of water buffalo bearing down on them. Panic-stricken by the anger of the elements, the wild animals were rushing madly through the low-growing scrub in a cloud of dust.

'They're coming straight for us!' gasped Dorton in horror. 'Let's get out of here!'

'Wait!' snapped Brandon. 'We'll never make it in time.'

The herd, numbering fifteen or so of the massive cattle, was now less than fifty yards distant. They were spread out on a wide front, running parallel with the very edge of the deep ravine. To have fled across their path would be asking for death.

'Stay where you are!' Brandon ordered harshly. 'Get right to the edge of the drop. They may miss us by a few feet. If they don't, it'll be too bad!'

The herd came on, spurred to even greater madness by another rumbling earth explosion in the distance.

Standing less than a yard from the edge of the ravine, the party lined out. Their faces were set and grim, for unless the terrified creatures veered away, it looked as if they would all be swept to their death in the drop at their backs.

The thunder of hooves was deafening. One enormous beast came charging straight at Brandon, who was nearest the herd. He prepared to jump for his life. Then, at the last moment, the impact of the bull's weight loosened earth and rock at the edge of the ravine. With a frightful bellow of fear, the animal sheared off, colliding with its nearest neighbour. The side of the ravine crumbled away. Not a yard from where Brandon and the others crouched, a minor landslide developed. Plunging and struggling, the buffalo went down with it.

How they saved themselves Brandon never knew; but just as the remainder of the panic-stricken herd thundered by, the very ground on which they stood began to slide from under their feet. Grovelling and clawing with their fingers and toes, they fought to save themselves from going down. Then the thunder of hoof beats was fading as the buffaloes disappeared, racing up the edge of the ravine in their terror.

Brandon found himself lying face downwards in the dirt, choking for breath in a cloud of dust. Inches behind him was a sheer drop. Litzgor was dangling over the edge, his fingers clutching at the roots of a stunted acacia bush. Charmaine and Dorton clung to each other, their legs over the edge, not daring to move. Only Scheki and Brandon himself were on solid ground.

With the greatest care, the two of them approached Litzgor. His position was the most precarious of all, for the soil around the roots of the acacia bush was crumbling and falling past his face. Lying down themselves, they secured a hold on his wrists and hauled him to safety. Then they turned their attention to Dorton and Charmaine.

'I never want to do *that* again!' said Dorton presently. 'Give me an earthquake any time!'

'Come on,' urged Brandon. 'We still have to catch up to the others.'

'My invention,' added Litzgor firmly.

Brandon bit back the words he had been on the point of saying. They set off again, thankful to be alive and more determined than ever to overtake their enemies.

It was not until three hours later that they first sighted Raoul and Connic ahead of them. Cobra Crag reared its ugly head in the background, shimmering unsteadily against the blazing noon sky, its summit crowned by a pinkish-coloured cloud of volcanic fumes and dust from the ruptured earth around it.

'There they are!' cried Dorton excitedly. 'Hurry up, everyone. This is going to be the big clash!'

Brandon smiled sourly. He felt in no fit state to clash with anyone at the moment.

They pressed on at a faster pace now, for in spite of their weariness it was imperative to overtake Raoul and his companion. What would happen when they did, even Brandon did not know. Time would tell and circumstances guide them.

Leading the way with Scheki, Brandon

gradually outdistanced the remainder of the party. Dorton held back because of Charmaine, who was almost exhausted. Jan Litzgor was limping badly from a twisted ankle. Brandon and Scheki thrust on, closing the distance which separated them from the dragging figures of Raoul and Connie. Both appeared to be hard put to it to keep up any speed.

Raoul, turning his head, saw Brandon coming when he was still a hundred yards away. The sight of the avenging man who was bearing down on him put wings to Raoul's feet. He and Connie broke into a staggering run, weaving in and out among the broken ground and swampy patches that beset their path.

Then someone shouted from behind Brandon. He looked back anxiously, to see that Dorton was gesticulating wildly and pointing to the east. A glance in that direction showed Brandon a mass of fully armed and hostile natives approaching at a run. They were still a good half-mile away, coming down a slope towards a broad swamp. Brandon's jaw hardened at the sight, for it heralded trouble with a vengeance.

Scheki, catching sight of the approaching enemy, muttered something beneath his breath as he stumbled along.

'They're out for blood!' grunted Brandon grimly. 'They must think we're the cause of all this volcanic disturbance. This is bad, Scheki!'

'*Yebbo, inkosi*.' He kept on moving.

Suddenly Raoul and Connie halted in their tracks. By now Brandon and Scheki were close behind them. Brandon saw at a glance the reason for their stopping. Right across their path ran a deep fissure filled to the top with slowly flowing liquid mud, steaming and bubbling with sulphurous heat.

Scheki gave a yell of triumph. He halted and raised the spear he carried, flinging it with all his might at Raoul. The man gave a choking cry of fear as the blade struck the lower part of his arm. Then he turned to face Brandon, who put all his strength into a final sprint to reach the man. But Raoul was cornered and prepared to fight for his life. From his belt he drew a long hunting knife wrested from one of the natives during their escape bid earlier on. Brandon, too, had a knife. The two men watched each other warily, starting to circle on the brink of the fissure. Heat fanned up and made their vision swim.

Scheki gave a shout and darted off along the side of the fissure, chasing Connie, who had taken a chance and fled. From the corner of his eye Brandon saw Scheki slip and fall, clawing at the ground to save himself from going into the mud. Then he was on his feet again, going after Connie. But by now she had plunged into a thicket of jungle and was lost to view.

At almost the same moment, Raoul made his bid to kill Brandon with a desperate attack. Brandon met the lunging drive of his knife, parrying it with his arm against the man's outflung wrist. The keen edge of the blade seared his skin before being turned. He whipped back, flicking Raoul with the knife as he did so. Then Raoul, snarling like a trapped animal, flung himself on Brandon again. Brandon stretched out his left arm and fastened his fingers on Raoul's throat, gripping tightly. The man's knife sliced through the sleeve of his shirt as he strove to get home. Brandon drove his own knife deep in Raoul's side but missed his heart. Raoul let out a scream, staggering aside under the impact of the blow. The knife was almost wrenched from Brandon's grasp as the man's body writhed in agony. Raoul broke free with a sudden frenzied twist as Brandon prepared for the death blow. Blood flecked his lips and dribbled from the corner of his mouth as he panted for breath, half doubled with pain. But his eyes were feverishly bright as he came in at Brandon again, determined even though mortally wounded to kill his enemy. Brandon met the rush with the knife. Raoul's weapon raked the flesh of his ribs, stinging with a sudden burning pain. Brandon gasped, then his arm was forced backwards by the weight of Raoul's body against the knife. With a short scream the man stumbled forward, dragging the knife from Brandon's fingers. Buried to the hilt in his stomach, it was wrenched away. Raoul dropped his own knife, clutching and clawing at the hilt in a fruitless effort to draw it out. Brandon stood still, his eyes fixed on the weaving figure as it staggered blindly towards the edge of the bubbling mud river. He made no attempt to stop the dying man; indeed, he did not have the strength to, for swift reaction weakened him so that he almost dropped himself.

Raoul gave one last choking gasp and pitched headlong over the edge of the fissure. Brandon watched his writhing body slowly engulfed and swallowed. He felt no trace of pity at the sight.

Dorton, Litzgor and Charmaine arrived in time to see the last of Raoul. But no one was anxious to linger. The horde of approaching natives prompted them to move on quickly. A glance showed Brandon that the natives must go round a swamp before reaching them.

'Come on!' he shouted, setting off at a stumbling run in the direction taken by Scheki and Connie. 'We'll make it if we hurry.'

Some of the natives paused in their rush, bending their bows and sending a shower of arrows across the swamp towards them. Most fell short, but Brandon urged his companions on to greater speed. There was a definite danger that they would be cut off, for the natives were heading round the swamp in such a manner as to bring themselves down on Brandon's flank as they skirted the edge of the ravine. Racing on, barely capable of keeping their feet, the four people glanced across at the natives.

'They'll get us!' gasped Charmaine in a strangled whisper. 'They'll get us, Mike!'

He grabbed her wrist and fairly dragged her over the ground, but it was gradually becoming apparent that the running horde of natives would almost certainly round the swamp at about the same time as Brandon's party reached the end of it. Yet there was nothing for it but to carry on. It was useless to turn back now.

Brandon, leading the run, was gravely worried at the danger. It was now obvious that the natives would cut them off as they sped after Scheki and Connie. Only a miracle could save them from the slaughter, and even Brandon was not sanguine enough to think it possible.

More arrows flashed through the air,

landing thickly around them. Mercifully no one was hit, but the range was shortening rapidly, only a long arm of the mud swamp separating them from their enemies. Nor could Brandon retreat and widen the gap, for he and his friends were already on the very edge of the mud ravine where Raoul had perished.

Some of the natives were actually ahead of them now, the tongue of the swamp barely twenty yards wide between them. Brandon gritted his teeth and shouted encouragement to the others, though he felt in his heart that their time was up. Only that elusive miracle . . .

When it happened it very nearly wiped them all out.

The natives were yelling and screaming as they saw the moment of triumph approaching. Every yard they covered took them closer to the people they imagined had caused the utter ruin and devastation of their kraal. The gold god would be avenged! Death would come to the whites!

Then the simmering surface of the swamp began to burst and explode in a swift volcanic cataclysm. Boiling mud and steam geysered upwards, darkening the sky as the earth shook and shuddered underfoot.

Brandon gasped a warning, covering his head and face with his arms as he staggered blindly onwards. Fearful cries came from the terrified natives. They were caught on the very fringe of the eruption, many of them perishing in a ghastly bath of scalding mud and water. Brandon himself and his friends did not escape unscathed, though they were further from the centre of the quake by a good many yards. Hot mud and filth showered down on them as they raced ahead with renewed speed. In a fever of fear from which none of them was entirely devoid, they struggled to escape from the scaring heat of the mud. And when at length they were temporarily out of range, they sank to the ground exhausted, thankful to be alive after passing so close to death.

Of the natives there was now no sign. The majority of them had been swamped and wiped out by the fountain of mud and steam. Any survivors were too terrified to keep up their attack. Turning to flee from death, they were quickly lost to sight in the scrub. And still the surface of the swamp belched upwards in jagged waves and spurts of heat.

Brandon permitted his companions a brief rest before going on. In spite of all they had gone through, there was still the question of Connie to be settled. He hoped that Scheki would have overtaken her, but since there was no sign of him it was difficult to tell what had happened.

With the ground still heaving and shaking under their feet, and the swamp behind them bubbling furiously from the renewed heat of the underground disturbance, the party pressed on towards the stark rock of Cobra Crag. It was not until they had almost reached it and were in view of its base that they sighted Scheki and Connie.

Brandon halted abruptly, staring in wonderment. Then he started forward again more swiftly than ever. Dorton and Litzgor swore beneath their breath, but Charmaine was too weary to make a sound. It was all she could do to keep up with the others. If it hadn't been for

Mike, she'd have been left behind.

Scheki shouted urgently to Brandon as they raced towards him. He was standing on the edge of a smoking fissure, cut off from Connie, who was running for her life with a fast-moving river of molten mud not many yards behind. Brandon halted at Scheki's side, panting for breath. The rest of them gathered round.

'She'll never get away!' said Litzgor. 'And she's still got my gold locator.'

With geysers of mud and steam breaking out through the surface of the riven ground in her rear, Connie fled towards Cobra Crag. Brandon could not have reached her if he'd tried, for giant cracks were opening in the earth between them. Her only chance of survival was to reach the sanctuary of the crag.

They watched in a kind of fascination, wondering whether the fleeing figure would outstrip the quake or be swallowed by its torment. '*Bwana*,' whispered Scheki, 'she is there!' Connie made the base of the crag as a seething tide of mud and boiling water swept over the ground where she'd been but a moment before.

As they watched, they saw her scrambling up the lower rocks of the crag in a desperate effort to escape.

Brandon's mouth was hard and tight as he stared through the rising haze of steam and fumes. He swayed unsteadily to the quiver of the ground. Then Charmaine gasped and covered her face with her hands. Connie, already twenty or thirty feet up the steeply sloping side of the crag, had stopped. She peered downwards as a violent concussion made the very crag itself writhe in a tumult of broken rock. An instant later the watchers heard a thin, long-drawn scream above the din of the earthquake. For a split second the figure of Connie was outlined against the face of the crag, then very slowly it started falling, turning over and over in a sickening fashion as she struck rocks in her fall.

Brandon kept his eyes on the falling figure till it disappeared in the mist of steam and spouts of mud at the base of the crag. He said nothing as he turned away. Dorton had his arm round Charmaine's shoulder. Scheki's face was immobile. Litzgor stared unseeingly at Cobra Crag.

'I can build another locator,' he muttered.

Brandon squared his aching shoulders with an effort. 'If we stay where we are, we shan't build anything!' he said with sudden vehemence. 'We shan't even get out alive unless we look sharp.'

They pulled themselves together, turning from Cobra Crag and setting their faces towards civilisation. There were still many dangers across their path, but they started out with lighter hearts than they had known for several days. 'I'm coming back here one day,' said Dorton, surprisingly.

'Why?' asked Brandon.

Dorton shot a sidelong glance at Charmaine. 'There's a little matter of that golden idol,' he said quietly. 'It must be worth a king's ransom, and I think I'll be needing a wedding present soon.'

Brandon grinned, seeing the swift expression on Charmaine's face. Scheki gave a knowing smile as they reached the fringe of the quake zone and plunged into jungle terrain that was friendly by comparison.

We do hope that you have enjoyed reading this large print book.

Did you know that all of our titles are available for purchase?

We publish a wide range of high quality large print books including:
**Romances, Mysteries, Classics**
**General Fiction**
**Non Fiction and Westerns**

Special interest titles available in large print are:
**The Little Oxford Dictionary**
**Music Book, Song Book**
**Hymn Book, Service Book**

Also available from us courtesy of Oxford University Press:
**Young Readers' Dictionary**
**(large print edition)**
**Young Readers' Thesaurus**
**(large print edition)**

For further information or a free brochure, please contact us at:
**Ulverscroft Large Print Books Ltd.,**
**The Green, Bradgate Road, Anstey,**
**Leicester, LE7 7FU, England.**
**Tel:** (00 44) **0116 236 4325**
**Fax:** (00 44) **0116 234 0205**

# SOMETIMES THEY DIE

## Tony Gleeson

Detective Frank Vandegraf is familiar with acts of random violence during the committing of a crime; but the street robbery and death of a shady attorney gives him pause, as the victim seems to have been universally despised. As he struggles to make sense of a crime with not enough evidence and too many suspects, he finds he's been assigned a new partner. But before they can acclimatize to each other, the discovery of troubling new information relating to another unsolved assault and robbery will test their ability to work together.

# THE MISSING NEWLYWEDS

## Steven Fox

Sergeant Sam Holmes and Doctor Jamie Watson have been given what should be a simple case of finding a couple of newlyweds and their limo driver, who disappeared between their wedding reception venue and hotel. Holmes and Watson are puzzled as to why they would be kidnapped without a ransom being asked. On learning that the bride's deceased first husband was an operative for a large private investigative firm who was killed by a drunk driver, they begin to wonder if the case is not part of a wider conspiracy . . .

# PRISONER OF KELSEY HOUSE

## V. J. Banis

After her ailing, domineering mother dies, Jennifer is invited by relatives she never knew she had to visit them at Kelsey House. But her car stalls on the way there, and the house itself is an eerie old rambling place where it's all too easy to get lost. What's more, every so often a group of ghostly figures dances what might be a child's game, or a primitive rite, on the lawn. What is the secret of Kelsey House and its strange inhabitants — and will Jennifer escape with her life?

# MURDER ON LONDON UNDERGROUND

## Jared Cade

Peter Hamilton, London Underground's managing director, is horrified when his ex-wife is pushed under a train. Following the murder of a second commuter, he receives an anonymous phone call from an organization calling itself Vortex that is dedicated to preventing the privatization of the network: 'You were the intended victim . . . Next time you won't be so lucky.' Hamilton turns for help to Lyle Revel and Hermione Bradbury, a glamourous couple with a talent for solving murders. But as the death toll rises, the terrorists release a runaway train on the network . . .

# STING OF DEATH

## Shelley Smith

Devoted wife and mother Linda Campion is found dead in her hall, sprawled on the marble floor, clutching a Catholic medallion of Saint Thérèse. An accidental tumble over the banisters? A suicidal plummet? Or is there an even more sinister explanation? As the police investigation begins to unearth family secrets, it becomes clear that all was not well in the household: Linda's husband Edmund — not long home from the war — has disappeared; and one of their guests has recently killed himself . . .

# MRS. WATSON AND THE SHAKESPEARE CURSE

## Michael Mallory

London, 1906. One of the world's foremost Shakespeare scholars presents a paper at Madame Tussaud's which claims that the real author of the works accredited to the Bard of Avon was none other than Queen Elizabeth I. Few in his audience, including the redoubtable Amelia Watson, wife of Doctor John H., take him seriously — but shortly afterward he is found murdered in his hotel room. Worse — Amelia's actor friend, Harry Benbow, is falsely accused of the crime. Can Amelia clear his name before Scotland Yard catch up to him?

Books by Denis Hughes
in the Linford Mystery Library:

DEATH WARRIORS
FURY DRIVES BY NIGHT
DEATH DIMENSION
BLUE PERIL
MURDER FORETOLD
JUNGLE QUEST
MOUNTAIN GOLD

# BUSH CLAWS

On a geological expedition into dark-
est Africa, Rex Brandon encounters
two explorers, Litzgor and Dorton, both
suffering from malaria. Brandon admin-
isters medical aid, and on recovering,
the two men relate a fantastic tale.
Whilst prospecting in an unexplored
region, they had fled when attacked by
a hostile native tribe led by a white
woman with a mighty lion at her side.
Litzgor had dropped his new invention, an electronic box — now in the
hands of the mystery woman. Brandon
agrees to help, placing his expedition
in terrifying danger . . .